CAUGHT UP WITH THE CAPTAIN

A SMALL TOWN, SECOND CHANCE, SECRET
BABY, MILITARY ROMANCE

BAD BOY BAKERS
BOOK 5

KAIT NOLAN

TAKE THE LEAP PUBLISHING

A LETTER TO READERS

Dear Reader,

This book contains swearing and pre-marital sex between the lead couple, as those things are part of the realistic lives of characters of this generation, and of many of my readers.

If either of these things are not your cup of tea, please consider that you may not be the right audience for this book. There are scores of other books out there that are written with you in mind. In fact, I've got a list of some of my favorite authors who write on the sweeter side on my website at https://kaitnolan.com/on-the-sweeter-side/

If you choose to stick with me, I hope you enjoy!

Happy reading!

Kait

1

Shoulders hunched against the damp winter wind, Mitchell Greyson stepped inside Elvira's Tavern. As the heavy wood door swung shut behind him, cutting off the cold, he waited for his eyes to adjust. Though he hadn't set foot in here for more than three decades, he still recognized shades of the place it used to be in the wooden booths built along the perimeter walls and the dark beams crossing the ceiling. But the floors had clearly been sanded down and refinished at some point. They glowed with the warmth of well-restored wood. The walls and ceiling had been repainted sometime after public smoking had been outlawed, covering up years of stains with a bright, warm cream. Somebody with a hell of a lot of talent had refaced the long bar with carved panels, and the shelves holding the selections of liquor were a subtle testament to someone who knew how to craft things out of wood for both function and beauty. Strands of garland and twinkle lights along the shelves and around some of the supporting columns were the only real nod to the holiday season. The whole place was warm and inviting, more elevated and subtly sophisticated than the merely functional bar and grill it had been during Grey's youth. Given tourism had finally made its way to Eden's Ridge, he figured that was a positive.

The man he'd come to meet was already seated in a corner booth, his back to the wall where he could observe the whole place.

Once a SEAL, always a SEAL.

Grey unwound his scarf and strode across the tavern to join him. "Ferguson."

"Captain." Jonah's tone was cool, respectful, but Grey could see a hint of temper in his familiar green eyes. He'd expected that.

Shucking his coat, he slipped into the opposite side of the booth. "Thank you for coming."

Jonah inclined his head. "Of course."

"You didn't have to. I'm not your CO anymore." And neither of them was still in the Navy.

A trace of amusement leaked into his expression. "Yeah, well, old habits are hard to break. You said you wanted to talk to me."

Grey opened his mouth to speak, but a cheerful voice with a broad East Tennessee twang broke in.

"What can I get you, fellas?" The well-endowed blonde flashed an extra bright smile at Jonah and made Grey feel about twice his fifty-three years.

He lifted a brow at the younger man. "Let me buy you a beer?"

"All right. I'll have a glass of that IPA on tap."

"I'll have the same."

"Any appetizers? Or would you like to go ahead and order dinner?"

Depending on how this conversation went, they probably wouldn't be here that long. "That's all for now."

"Coming right up."

She sashayed away, the extra swing in her step entirely lost on the very-engaged Jonah, who barely spared her a glance.

Not in the habit of mincing words, Grey took a breath and dove in. "I wanted to apologize for last month."

One dark brow lifted. "Just for last month?"

Damn, he looked just like his mother when he did that. Had it always been that pronounced, or had being home and back around her on a regular basis brought more of those expressions to the surface?

"I didn't show up at your business intending to blindside you. I really did come to check and see how you were doing."

After a head injury ended his naval career, Jonah had completed an experimental therapy program that trained him as a master baker. He'd returned home with two friends from the same program and opened a bakery.

"So seeing my mom there was just a bonus?" On the surface, his tone was conversational, but there was a thrum of something underneath that Grey couldn't quite peg.

Seeing Rebecca there had been... shocking. Exciting. And, in its own way, devastating.

"She was part of the business that brought me to town, but I had no way of knowing she'd be there that day."

"And if she hadn't been, would you ever have told me you two knew each other?"

That was the crux of the younger man's irritation. Grey could respect it. "Eventually. Look, I know you're pissed I kept it from you that I was from here. That I knew your mom. But I had my reasons. You and I had a professional relationship. Rebecca and I didn't part on good terms." *Understatement of the century.* "I had no idea what she might say about me if you went home and asked, and I didn't want that to damage our working relationship, or the mutual respect we were building. Add to that, I didn't want anybody to accuse me of favoritism."

A furrow dug in between Jonah's brows. "Favoritism?"

"I didn't exactly favor you, but I kept a closer eye on you than I would have. Because you were hers, and because she mattered to me." Once upon a time, he'd have done anything for Rebecca Ferguson.

Anything except the one thing she'd wanted.

The server came back with their beers. "Anything to eat, y'all?"

They both shook their heads, and she retreated.

Jonah lifted his glass and sipped before leaning back in his seat. "What's the deal with you two? Mom got weird after you were here last month."

Grey wondered what kind of weird. "Well, that is largely between me and your mother. But I can tell you we were friends for years. She and your dad and I were the three amigos from the time we were little. All the way back to about the second grade."

But they hadn't stayed that way. It seemed inevitable now that he and Lonnie would both have fallen in love with her.

Sipping at his own beer, Grey fought not to fall into the past. "After high school, your mom and I had a big fight. We both said things we probably regretted, and I haven't seen her in over thirty years. Until that day at the bakery. I've certainly had time to grow up and think about how things might've been different, and I'm sure she has, too. We've got some history we need to work through, and that's just for us. But I know my coming back here impacts you, too, and I wanted to say I'm sorry for not telling you. I wouldn't change my decision, but I understand that the whole situation was probably weird for you."

Jonah sat with that for a moment before nodding in acknowledgment. "I appreciate that." He leaned forward, elbows on the table. "So you're really moving back here now that you've retired?"

"That's the plan. I've been away from home for a long time. I'd like to come back."

"Why didn't you before?"

"My parents moved while I was in college. When I was on leave, I generally went to them." It had been both a blessing and a curse to have a reason to stay away from Tennessee and all the what ifs that lingered here.

"So, what are you going to *do?* You're not exactly the settle gracefully into puttering around kind of guy."

Grey snorted a laugh. That was putting it mildly. "You're not wrong. I got out about eight months ago. Went through this veteran transition training program out in Montana. It made a big difference, so I decided I want to open a similar program here. Or as close to here as I can manage. You know as well as I do that there will never be enough of those kinds of resources."

"True that. What about your family?"

"None left. I lost my dad about five years ago. Mom last year. I recently finished dealing with the cleaning out of their house and closing out of their estate, so it was a good time for a major change."

A shadow crossed Jonah's features. "Yeah. That shit's tough. I just did the same."

That was another point of pain for Grey. The man who'd once been a brother to him had died, and Grey had never once attempted to mend their relationship. Lonnie had gotten the girl, so Grey hadn't known how. Even when he'd found out from Jonah that his mom was divorced, he hadn't been able to make himself reach out. It was just one of many regrets he carried.

Jonah twitched his shoulders, as if shaking off his own dark thoughts. "So, what are you doing for Christmas?"

A fair question since it was the day after tomorrow.

"Nothing. It's just another day this year."

The younger man's face twisted in true horror. "No. Are you gonna be in town?"

"Yeah. I rented a house for the foreseeable future until I decide what I'm buying."

"Then you're coming to Christmas dinner."

Grey smiled a little, proud of this piece of military culture. Leave no man behind. "I appreciate the offer, but that's not necessary."

Jonah's mouth twisted into a familiar stubborn set that had Grey thinking about Rebecca again. "Absolutely not an option. You are not going to be alone on Christmas."

It wasn't like he was looking forward to it. But what Jonah was proposing wasn't as simple a thing as he made it out to be.

"Is this going to be okay with your mother?"

"We've always had an open door policy. She believes the more the merrier. And as you said, y'all used to be friends."

Friends was the least of what they'd been, but he wasn't going to mention that to Rebecca's son. Because of that history, he wasn't sure this was the best idea. But he wanted the chance to get close to her again, and he wouldn't waste the opportunity presented.

"Well, all right then. Just tell me when and where and what I can bring."

"YOU'RE LOOKING AWFULLY cheerful for a woman about to be feeding sixteen people."

Rebecca Ferguson grinned and linked her arm with Donna Black, one of her long-time friends. "All my chicks are home to roost, so I'm especially thankful."

There'd been too many years of quiet Christmases while Jonah had been deployed, when it had only been her and her daughter, Samantha. Now Jonah was free of the Navy and here with his soon-to-be wife, Rachel. Sam was here with her husband, Griff, and their baby girl, Rory, the absolute love of Rebecca's life. And as if that wasn't bounty enough, all the extended, adopted family that came along with Bad Boy Bakers was here, too. Both of Jonah's business partners, Brax and Holt, whom she'd informally adopted as soon as they moved to town, their wives and children, and a handful of others linked to them, including Donna, Holt's mother-in-law. Finding seating was proving to be a challenge, but Rebecca wouldn't have it any other way.

"No, no, shove the sofa against the far wall. That should give you room for the extra tables you brought from the bakery."

"We've gotta move all of Rory's Christmas presents first," Jonah announced. "I'm not sure why you went so nuts buying her stuff. She's only six months old. She's not gonna remember all this."

Rebecca shot a mock scowl at her son. "Oh hush, you. Don't you rain on my grandma parade."

"That's right," Donna agreed. "Spoiling our grandchildren is one of our greatest joys in life."

Holt shot a significant glance at his wife that nobody missed.

Cayla pressed her lips together to hide a smile. "Then I suppose this is as good a time as any to let y'all know you're getting another one."

Donna's mouth fell open. "You're pregnant?"

Cayla nodded, brown eyes twinkling.

The general volume rose several decibels as all the women began to squee and rushed forward to hug the mom-to-be.

Holt's younger sister Hadley rested a hand on her own barely visible baby bump. "Oh, thank God. I won't be the only one living off limeade and ginger ale."

"The morning sickness really hasn't been that bad this go-round."

Hadley grimaced. "I hate you a little bit right now."

Her fiancé, Cash, tugged her back against him, pressing a kiss to the top of her head. "Yours is getting better."

"I do think I can safely fall on that Christmas feast in there like a pack of ravening wolves, so there's that."

"Speaking of food, everything's more or less ready," Rachel announced. "We should probably start getting hands washed and drinks poured while the guys finish setting up the tables."

A joyful chaos ensued, and Rebecca soaked up every minute. There was nothing better than family, be they of the blood or of the heart.

In less than twenty minutes, the extra tables had been set up in the living room to make one long table. Cayla had put her event planner skills to work and fitted them out with runners, centerpieces, placemats, and cloth napkins folded into some kind of fancy pinwheel. Rebecca had put her foot down on the china. No one wanted to do that many dishes by hand. The high-quality paper plates would be just fine.

The doorbell rang as Rebecca was lighting the final candle. She glanced around, confused. "Did somebody get locked out?"

"Oh, yeah." Jonah scrubbed a hand over his head. "I forgot to tell you. I invited one more."

"Oh." She couldn't be frustrated. This had always been her rule. They'd make room for one more. But she wished he'd thought to tell her while they were still sorting the seating. "Well, go let them in." She turned to the tables, wondering where the hell they were going to shoehorn one more person in. Maybe if they shifted the high chair, they could wedge someone on the end down near her.

At the sound of more footsteps, she turned to greet the newcomer and felt the words die on her lips as she spotted him. All the chaos of parents wrangling kids faded into the background, and time seemed to slow as he stepped into the room and sucked up all the oxygen. Though silver threaded through his dark hair and beard, the years had been more than kind to Grey. A lifetime in the Navy had kept him fit, and she recognized the same economy of motion and readiness of stance she saw in her son.

He'd promised last month that he'd be seeing her. That he was coming home. But she hadn't believed him. Just like she hadn't been able to trust that he would come back when she was eighteen. A potent mix of joy and anxiety crawled through her as the corner of his mouth tipped up in a hesitant smile. The smile she'd missed like hell for years.

"Hey, Rebel."

His voice was a deeper rasp now, but the tone was the same, full of affection and humor and the shared secrets of someone who'd once known her down to the ground. No one had ever called her that but him, and she'd loved it, as much as she'd once loved him. Hearing it now erased thirty-odd years of life and longing, leaving her feeling far more like an addled teenager than a brand-new grandmother.

"Grey." She'd have preferred to sound a lot more carefree and breezy, but at this point, she was proud to have found her voice at all. "Welcome."

Breaking contact with the hazel eyes she'd once known as well as her own, she began snapping orders.

"Griff, go grab the desk chair from Sam's room. We'll figure out where to slot it in at the tables."

"Yes, ma'am."

"Rachel, do we have enough silverware?"

"I'll grab another set."

"Donna, can you fill another glass with ice?"

Her friend was already reaching for the cabinet above the dishwasher.

When Rebecca turned back, Grey was *right there*, close enough to touch. She looked up at him, remembering what it had felt like to hug him again after so many years. She hadn't been able to stop herself when she'd seen him in the bakery. No matter how complicated their history, nothing had been able to override that desire in the moment. Nerves were the only thing stopping her right now, because his presence here was like dancing around a bunch of land mines.

"I brought wine. And a little gift for the hostess."

"Oh, I—" She accepted the bottle, and the large gift bag. "Thank you."

He searched her face, lowering his voice. "If this isn't okay, I can leave. I gather Jonah didn't tell you I was coming."

"He didn't, no." And what would she have done if he had? "It's just a surprise, is all."

Those eyes that had always seen too much stayed on hers. "I don't want to make this awkward for you. I know we didn't part on the most positive terms."

Pain lanced through her at the memory of the things they'd both said out of heat and hurt. "It was a long time ago. Water under the bridge." It had to be, because she couldn't think about all that right now. Digging up a smile, she laid a hand on his arm and admitted the truth she could tell him. "I am happy to see you, Grey. Please stay."

He covered her hand with his and squeezed, sending a buzz of electricity all the way up her arm. "I'd like that."

2

From the time they'd been little, Rebecca had always wanted a big family. Grey had assumed that was because she was an only child, only grandchild, and the end of the line for both sides of her family. Looking around the jam-packed room, at all the people laughing and eating, he realized she'd absolutely gotten her wish. It might've been unconventional, but it was clear that Jonah's business partners looked on her as every bit the mom Jonah did, and she doted on all their kids as well. Brax and Mia's little boy, who couldn't have been more than two or three, perched happily in her lap, inhaling the carefully cut bites of everything from her plate.

Grey shifted, and his knee brushed against Rebecca's. As the buzz of that contact seared up his leg, her gaze shot to his.

"Sorry," he murmured. He wasn't, really. They were all jammed in cheek-by-jowl, and though it had been an innocent touch, her reaction was exactly what he wanted to see. She'd felt something, too, and that gave him hope.

She shifted in her own chair, and her eyes slipped away, back to Duncan. There was something nervous about the move, and Grey wondered whether it was a good nervous or if his presence made her truly uncomfortable. She was too good a hostess to admit it.

Wanting to grant her a reprieve, he turned his attention to her daughter, who was seated to his left. "So, Sam, what is it you do?"

"I'm an English professor at a little private college in Chattanooga. And you're an old friend of Mom's?"

Her tone was perfectly polite, but he didn't miss the rampant curiosity in her brown eyes. They were shaped like Rebecca's, but the color was all Lonnie.

"And your dad's. We all went way back." He couldn't mention one without the other.

A complicated mix of emotions flitted across Sam's face, suggesting she'd had a complicated relationship with her father. He regretted saying anything to cause that flash of pain.

It was more than obvious to Grey that he'd never been talked about. Which was fine. There was no reason for Rebecca to have ever mentioned that they'd been involved, considering she'd married his best friend. The pang he felt at that was old and dull, an ache he'd long ago learned how to live with. He didn't have the right to be upset about it. He'd blown his shot with her, and that had been the end of that.

Except it hadn't been entirely the end. She'd divorced Lonnie years ago, well before he died. Grey wondered what had happened to destroy the happy picture they'd made. Now definitely wasn't the time or place to ask.

"So why Rebel? I've never heard anybody call Mom that."

"No one ever did but Grey."

Tuning back into the conversation, he met her eyes again. "You never told them that story?"

Her mouth tipped up in a half smile. "And give them ideas when they were growing up? No, thank you."

"Well, now you have to tell," Jonah insisted.

Rebecca shot her son a look. "Can't we just leave it that you didn't get your wild streak from your dad?"

"Oh, no. Spill, Captain."

Grey arched his brows at her, silently asking for permission. She rolled her eyes with a sigh. "Fine."

He waited for her to continue, but she just waved a hand in his direction. "You started this."

As all attention swung to him, Grey steepled his fingers. "Well, your mom was a bit of a wild child."

"I find this really hard to believe," Sam put in.

Had she really changed that much or was this simply a part of her life she'd elected to omit? He liked the idea that he knew a side of Rebel that no one else here did.

"No, really. In some groups, it's the girls who are the voices of reason, stopping the guys from doing something stupid or reckless. But your mom was right there with Lonnie and me, proving she could do everything we could, and do it better. She was fearless."

"I wasn't fearless. I just didn't want to get left behind."

There was something in her tone that made him wonder if she was talking about more than their group adventures.

"Anyway, are y'all familiar with Stockton Quarry Lake?"

Jonah frowned. "All the way down in Jericho? That's a haul. Isn't it private property?"

"Yep. Was back then, too. But that didn't stop us from sneaking past the fences to go hang out there."

"It's this gorgeous blue water so clear you can see all the way to the bottom. Well worth the hike in." Rebecca's tone was nostalgic.

"Good thing, as it was quite the hike. It's in the middle of at least three hundred acres of woods. Which we didn't know that first time."

"Lord, we had blisters for days from walking that far in flip-flops. Lonnie was so mad. He kept wanting to turn around, but I kept insisting it had to be just a little further."

Grey chuckled. "If you were gonna go to the trouble to break and enter, you were gonna see what you set out to see."

Her lips curved. "Heck yeah. If I was risking getting arrested, I wanted it to be worth it. And oh, it was."

"To you, anyway. You weren't the one who ended up with buckshot in your backside when the owner caught us all swimming out there." He shifted in his seat, as if the sting of the shot were still fresh.

She pressed her lips together in an effort to sober, but her green eyes danced with mirth. "I did apologize."

"You did. Didn't stop me from snarling at you the whole time you were doing field surgery to fish the pellets out. 'If you didn't have to be such a rebel, this never would have happened.'" Grey shrugged. "And the nickname just stuck. Not sure you got all that buckshot out, for the record."

"Well, that's what you get for thinking I could do field surgery with you laid out on the hood of a truck."

"Lonnie got sick at the sight of blood. You were definitely the better option."

They were grinning at each other by the time Grey registered that everyone else was staring.

Sam shook her head. "I... don't even know what to say about that."

Rebecca shrugged. "I was far more interesting in my younger years. Now, who wants dessert?"

A resounding chorus of affirmatives rang out around the table.

"Actually, before we do that, now is probably a good time to open that other thing I brought. It's kind of for everybody."

"Okay." With a not insignificant level of side-eye, Rebecca rose, passing Duncan to Mia.

She came back with the bag and sat, pulling out tissue

paper to reveal the contents. Her face lit up with surprise and joy as she pulled out the first box.

"Christmas crackers!" The smile she aimed his way made it worth the drive into Knoxville to track them down.

"I remember how much you used to love them."

"Are they cinnamon-flavored or something?" Griff asked.

"No, no. They're not food." Rebecca tore open a box and pulled out one of the crackers. "Let's show them how it works."

Grey dutifully took the other end of the twisted cardboard tube. "On three. One."

"Two."

"Three."

They both tugged, and the cracker made its signature *pop!* as it ripped apart. Grey ended up with the bigger portion of the tube.

"You won."

He pulled out the paper crown and unfolded it. "Well, obviously, there's only one person here who should wear a crown." Before he could think better of it, he settled the green paper crown on Rebecca's head.

She pursed her lips and flashed her pageant-ready smile. "Why thank you, kind sir."

That smile hit Grey right in the sternum. Blindly, he reached for the cracker and dumped the rest of the contents. His fingers closed on the slip of paper with the joke. "What do you get if you eat Christmas decorations?"

Eyes narrowed in consideration, Rebecca sat back. "I know I've heard this one before." She straightened, slapping a hand on the table. "Tinselitis!"

"Got it in one."

"That's terrible," Jonah declared.

"That's prime-time dad joke material," Holt argued.

Into it now, Rebecca leaned forward again, green eyes sparkling. "What's the novelty?"

"It seems we have ye classic Fortune Teller Fish."

She plucked it from his grasp, pulling out the card and the red cellophane fish from the bag and placing the latter in his outstretched hand.

Sam peered at the thing in his palm as it started to wriggle. "How's that supposed to work?"

"The fish moves and is supposed to tell you something about the person who's holding it," he explained.

"We used to have the best time with these. Okay, let's see. The tail is moving. And the head."

As they all watched, the thing curled up into a roll.

"That means Grey is—" She paused, consulting the card with the interpretations. Color rose in her cheeks and her gaze shot to his, her pupils blown wide.

Mia peered over her shoulder to read the answer. "Passionate."

Grey's skin caught fire with memory. The silence spun out way the hell too long, but he couldn't look away. She was frozen, eyes blurred with the same memories of a summer night a lifetime ago when everything had changed. He wanted to touch her. Wanted to lean forward and lay his lips over the rosy blush of hers to see if she tasted as he remembered. As if she could read his thoughts, her mouth parted.

"Those look like fun. Are there enough for everybody?"

Rachel's voice broke the spell. Rebecca dropped the card and reached into the bag. "Looks like. Here." She leaped up and passed out more of the crackers to everyone.

Keeping his movements unhurried, Grey exhaled a quiet breath and gulped down more tea to wet his parched throat. He watched as the others opened their crackers, laughed as they read the jokes, and pretended not to notice the long, assessing looks periodically shot his way. He ate the dessert, though he couldn't have said what it was on pain of death. And as little kid eyes began to droop, and the young families started gathering people up, he helped to clear the table.

"I can help with dish duty."

"That's not necessary. We've got it." But Rebecca's smile took any sting out of the refusal. She began walking toward the door, and he recognized it was time to leave.

"Thanks for having me." He shrugged into his coat. "It was nice not to spend the day alone, and good to see the family you've built. It's a great one."

"It is. They're great kids." She hesitated for a moment, then leaned in for a hug.

On a sigh, he wrapped his arms around her, soaking in the comfort he hadn't felt in all these years, other than the fleeting greeting she'd offered at the bakery last month. God, he'd missed everything about this. About her. She fit. Even after all these years, she fit. And the electric connection between them was still alive and well.

She pulled back, scooping a hand through her hair. "It's been great to see you."

"You, too. Merry Christmas, Rebel."

His last sight, as he trotted down her front walk, was of Rebecca framed in the doorway, arms folded against the cold, her cheeks pink, her hair stirring in the winter breeze. She was still there as he slid into his car. He lifted a hand in one last wave and started the engine.

He might have fucked up his first chance with her all those years ago, but he sure as hell wasn't going to screw up the second.

"I LOVE THE HOLIDAYS, but I'm so glad they're over." Jolene Lowrey punctuated the statement with a gusty sigh as Rebecca dug her fingers in for a thorough scalp massage while working shampoo through Jolene's hair.

"Are they over, though? There's always that sense of not quite resolved to me until after New Year's." Then again, Rebecca knew her own sense of anticipation this week had nothing to do with waiting for the clock to run down on this year.

"Fair enough, but all the family's gone home. I dearly love seeing them, but I'm always so glad to get my quiet back. My tolerance for chaos seems to go down every year."

Rebecca laughed. "I'm still happy enough to enjoy the chaos."

From across the shop, her business partner Candice looked up from the color she was applying to Jana Samson's roots. "You had a houseful this year, didn't you?"

Rebecca wrung out Jolene's hair and wrapped it in a towel, nudging her toward the chair at her station. "Oh yeah. Everybody was here for Rory's first Christmas. And of course, I consider Holt and Brax mine now, too, so they came in for dinner with their wives and kids. And Donna came, too."

She didn't mention the extra addition they'd had, but she'd sure as hell had Grey on her mind in all the days since, despite efforts to distract herself. "It was wonderful to have the house full of people, so it'll be another week or so before I'm grateful for the quiet. Sam and Griff headed home with the baby this morning. And Jonah and Rachel left for Syracuse the day after Christmas, to go spend some time with her family."

"Oh, how's the wedding planning going?" Jana asked.

Considering her daughter had gotten married in Vegas, and Jonah and Rachel wanted something small and intimate, Rebecca considered herself lucky that she hadn't had dreams of a big, ostentatious white wedding. God knew, she hadn't had that herself when she'd married Lonnie all those years ago. So long as everyone was happy, that was the only thing that mattered to her.

She combed out Jolene's hair and began the trim the older woman had come in for. "It's more or less settled. They're opting for a small ceremony down here. Mostly family and friends. We've got right at a month to go."

As everyone continued to discuss the wedding, she couldn't stop herself from wondering whether Grey would still be in Eden's Ridge by then. Jonah had mentioned he was renting a house somewhere in town. By all accounts, he was some version of back, but Rebecca didn't know what that meant or what it would look like, or even what to think about it. She didn't know what to think about that moment after dinner, with the Christmas crackers and the stupid fish. The air had felt electric, alive with memories she'd done her best to bury.

How she'd made it through the rest of the night, she didn't know. Some credit for that had to go to Rachel, who'd successfully distracted everyone with the rest of the Christmas crackers. She wondered whether her future daughter-in-law had picked up on the tension or if had been simply a lucky break. The entire interaction had made her feel spotlit. As if there were a blinking neon sign above their heads announcing *Former Lovers*.

That wasn't a conversation she wanted to have with her children.

But it had been impossible not to think about what it would feel like if he touched her. To wonder if he'd taste the same, or if memory had gilded reality with nostalgia. One thing was for damned sure—the man had far more potency than he'd possessed at eighteen. If he elected to point that in her direction again, she wasn't sure she could resist him. She didn't think she'd want to try.

The bell jangled as someone pushed open the door. Focus still on Jolene's trim, she called out, "Be with you in a minute."

Candice cleared her throat.

Rebecca looked up, checking the mirror to see who'd walked in. Her heart stuttered as she spotted Grey standing in the entryway. Almost as one, every woman in the shop sat up and took notice. And why shouldn't they? He was a fine specimen of a man, with those broad shoulders and that firm jaw. And when was the last time she'd noticed anything about a man beyond the cursory?

Because her hand felt weak, she dropped it, lest she inadvertently give Jolene a new style she hadn't asked for. Aware her pulse had kicked up with surprise and anticipation, she turned to face him fully. Of what she couldn't say, but every atom of her body was attuned to him. Because of that focus, she picked up on the slight stiffness in his posture, the wariness in his gaze. "Grey?"

Good Lord. Was she ever going to be able to greet him with more than just his name?

"Hey, Rebel. I wasn't sure if you took walk-ins or not." Those hazel eyes zeroed in on her, as if he didn't even notice all the other people in the room.

Her brain short-circuited, and she had no idea what to say.

Candice eased over, nudging her with an elbow. "Yes, she does."

Rebecca opened her mouth to inform him she needed to finish with Jolene, but Candice simply slipped the scissors from her fingers.

"You go on and take care of him. I've got Mrs. Lowrey. That's okay, right, hon?"

"Oh, yes," Jolene agreed.

Rebecca had the ridiculous thought that she should charge admission for this show. Swallowing hard, she searched for some professionalism. "Okay then. What are you looking for?"

He scooped a hand through his hair, causing the silver to catch the light. Damn, that worked for him. Her fingers itched to follow that path, to explore the feel and texture of how his hair had changed. He'd always had the best hair. Thick and soft and fun to play with.

"It's getting kind of long. I figured you could do a little cleanup."

Her lips curved. "You consider this long?" Back in high school, he'd had a ponytail, to the eternal horror of his parents.

With a self-conscious laugh, he came further into the shop, shrugging off his coat. "I left my pirate days behind a while ago. I got used to short hair in the Navy."

"Come on back. I'll wet you down."

He trailed her to the shampoo sink, sitting where she indicated and leaning his head back into the bowl. Because she could, she indulged herself, skimming her fingers through the strands. The texture was a little different. That was the nature of gray hair. But the bulk of it was still soft, still thick. Cutting too much off would be a crime.

Grey sighed at the touch, visibly relaxing under her hands and closing his eyes. For the first time, she wondered what weights he carried. Jonah had come back from his service with his fair share of darkness. Grey had been in for so much longer, finishing a full career, working his way up the ranks. How much of the things he'd seen and done now lived in his head, in his bones?

Wanting to lessen some of that burden, Rebecca turned on the water, wetting down his hair and working her fingers through to rub his scalp. So many people enjoyed the head massage that went along with washing hair. She'd performed exactly this service countless times in her career. But it had never felt this intimate before. As she began to work shampoo to a lather, he groaned. The soft, low sound of pleasure reached inside her, unlocking and igniting a whole host of memories she'd been trying hard not to think about.

Yep, she needed to finish this part, cut his hair, and scoot him on out of the shop so she could find her equilibrium again.

Drawing on all her professionalism, she rinsed his hair and draped a towel along the back of his neck. "Just head on over to that chair, there." She'd borrow Candice's station for this, since Jana was under the dryer just now.

Grey lowered himself into the chair, meeting her eyes again in the mirror. Nope. She couldn't keep catching glimpses of those eyes and wondering what the hell he was thinking. So she turned the chair away from the mirror.

"Do you trust me?"

He waited a beat too long to reply. "Always."

Choosing not to analyze what he might've meant by that, she grabbed her scissors and comb and went to work. It was easier to lose herself in the job, to simply focus on shape and lines, and what would best accent that wonderful face. He stayed silent through the whole process, letting her do her thing, and she was grateful. The girls would have enough to talk about after he left, without him inadvertently revealing more about their past.

Crouching partly in front of him, she angled his head this way and that, checking her work. Satisfied with the end result, she straightened. With brisk, efficient movements, she brushed the hair off his neck and shoulders and removed the cape before turning him to face the mirror. "What do you think?"

"I think you should have dinner with me."

If she'd been holding a bottle of product, she'd have bobbled it. "What?"

"Have dinner with me so we can have a proper catch up without the risk of spilling secrets to your kids." His eyes glinted with humor. "Since apparently they have no idea what a wild child you used to be."

It was a terrible idea. Some part of her knew that. But her

brain was blanking on a reason to refuse. At least any she could admit to in front of an audience.

When she said nothing, he lifted a brow. "Are you busy tomorrow night?"

Candice spoke up from the shampoo bowl, where she'd taken Jana to rinse off her color. "Nope. She's completely free."

Rebecca shot her a Look. Really? Did she have to say it like that? As if she didn't have an actual life or options?

But it was the truth. She couldn't think of a single reason to say no. And there was a part of her that wanted what he offered. The chance to actually talk to him, away from the kids. Away from everybody else. They needed to clear the air. She needed to apologize for the things she said in anger back when they'd last seen each other.

With whatever shreds of dignity she could muster, she folded the cape. "I find myself with the evening free."

He shoved up from the chair and turned to face her, stepping close enough she had to tip her head back to meet his eyes. "Okay. I'll pick you up at six."

"Fine. See you then."

One corner of his mouth kicked up as he dropped several bills on the corner of her station. "See you tomorrow, Rebel."

The women in the shop at least waited until he was out of view of the front window before they broke into a collective squee.

"Girl! Who is that gorgeous hunk of man?" Candice wanted to know. "You obviously know each other."

"Oh, that's Mitchell Greyson," Jolene said. "I went to church with his parents back in the day, before they moved. That was a long time ago, though."

"More than thirty years," Rebecca murmured. "We were friends a long time ago."

"Looks like he's got more than friends on his mind now," Candice crowed.

"And you've got a date with *him* for New Year's Eve?" Jana asked. "Lucky girl."

"Wait. What? Tomorrow's New Year's Eve?" Rebecca turned back to the window, as if her will alone was enough to draw him back.

A date on New Year's came with a certain expectation. Didn't it? It was bigger. More important, somehow.

She thought of that half smirk. He'd known it, too. Damn him.

Well, it was too late now. She didn't have his number, and she wouldn't call Jonah to try to get it from him. Not on pain of death. She'd just have to suck it up and deal.

Stepping toward the mirror, she inspected her roots. The silver accents might look great on him, but she wasn't quite ready to bow to Mother Nature yet. "Candice, do you have time to squeeze me in to touch up my roots?"

"Girl, I will make time. But here's the better question: What on earth are you going to wear?"

3

As he strode up Rebecca's front walk, it occurred to Grey that he'd never done this before—picked her up for a formal date. Back in high school, they'd just been friends, and when things had changed between them that last summer, they'd kept everything on the down-low because they'd both worried about how Lonnie would react to the shift in their group dynamic. It felt good to go straight up to her door, no worries about friends or parents. But there were still plenty of nerves around the woman herself. She didn't yet understand his intentions. That he was well and truly in this for a second chance.

But she would. And Grey was determined not to fuck it up.

He rang the bell at six on the dot. The front door swung open almost at once, as if she'd been waiting just on the other side. The sight of her distracted him from his pleasure over the idea that she'd anticipated this night as much as he had. His breath wooshed out. The deep purple of the wrap dress she wore made those stunning green eyes pop, and it clung to her curves in a way that made his hands itch to touch and explore. Her rich brown hair fell in stylish, glossy waves around her shoulders, framing the face that had always stolen his breath. She'd done something with makeup he couldn't have identified, but it enhanced rather than concealed. She'd always been beautiful, and the intervening years had done nothing to diminish that. Objectively, he knew she'd had two children. That she was technically a grandmother now. But he couldn't see any of that as he looked at her. He saw only a vital, vibrant, attractive woman that he wanted on every possible level.

Down, boy.

Swallowing hard, he found a smile. "You look amazing."

Rebecca smoothed a self-conscious hand down her skirt. "Is this okay? You didn't tell me where we were going, so I had to guess."

"Actually, I figured you'd appreciate not being the center of gossip, so if it's alright with you, I'm cooking back at my place."

She loosed a breath, her shoulders dropping to a more relaxed posture as she slipped into her coat. "Thank you. That's great. You left quite the ruckus in the hen house yesterday."

He waited for her to lock the door behind her and offered his arm. "In retrospect, asking you out at your place of business was maybe not my best move. But I didn't have your phone number."

When she hesitated, he wondered if he'd made a mistake clarifying right off that he intended this to be a date, not just a catch up between old friends.

But she slipped her arm through his. "I expect we should rectify that."

He curled his fingers over hers, soaking in the warmth from that point of contact. "We should."

The drive back to his rental house took only a few minutes. He let her inside and led her back to the kitchen, where he'd left a bottle of wine and two glasses. As she peeled off her coat, he pulled the charcuterie board he'd prepped out of the fridge and set it on the counter beside the bowl of crackers before opening the wine and pouring her a glass.

Rebecca lifted a brow as she accepted. "I'm impressed."

"I've got a little more game than I had at eighteen."

Her rich laugh echoed through the kitchen as he poured his own glass.

"Please, sit. I'll get started on dinner."

She slid onto one of the barstools and assembled a stack of salami and one of the fancy cheeses. "I feel like we need to address the elephant in the room."

Grey paused, his hands fisting on the container of baby bella mushrooms. Was she really going to put everything right out there? "All right."

"First off, I need to say that I'm so sorry for all the hurtful things I said the last time I saw you. I was young and angry, and I didn't know how to deal with the fact that you and I weren't on the same page. That whole summer, I was building a life for us in my head, but I didn't actually talk to you about it."

"And then I went and built a different one."

She lifted her glass in acknowledgment. "It wasn't fair of me to get angry about that."

"I get it. And I didn't win any prizes for how I handled things either. As you say, we were young, and, really, probably not ready for what we found." God knew, he hadn't understood what he'd walked away from then. But he didn't want to linger in a past that couldn't be changed. "How about we both acknowledge we hurt each other, and we both regret it?"

"I can accept that."

They toasted the long overdue detente.

"What was the other thing? You said that was first."

"Oh, well, there's the issue of Jonah."

Pulse beating thick in his veins, Grey deliberately didn't pick up the knife. "What about him?"

"Why didn't you tell him you knew me?"

So it wasn't what he suspected. Or if it was, she was staying quiet for now. Grabbing a kitchen towel, he began to clean the mushrooms. "As I mentioned, I was Jonah's CO for several years. In that capacity, I needed to have a particular kind of relationship with him that wasn't clouded by any personal stuff. I had no idea what your reaction might be if he brought me up, so I kept it under my hat. Over the years, we got to be pretty close. Your son is loyal as the day is long, and frankly, I didn't want to lose that by bringing our complicated past into it. Especially since I had no way of knowing if I'd ever even been mentioned. Which, I'm guessing, I wasn't."

Distress flickered over her pretty face.

"That's not a criticism, Rebel. You married Lonnie. There was no reason for you to have told your kids about me. But I have wondered for years why Jonah's a Ferguson and not a Barker."

"Well, that's a story."

He wouldn't press her, but he waited, letting the silence do the job for him as he continued to chop vegetables.

Rebecca spun her wineglass, staring into its depths, as if the words she needed were hiding in the deep red liquid. "I don't know if you were aware that Lonnie and I divorced well before he died."

"Yeah. Jonah mentioned something at one point." And it had killed Grey not to interrogate him about it. He'd wanted to know everything, but there was no reasonable or graceful way to ask without getting into truths he hadn't been prepared to reveal. He picked up the knife and began to slice the mushrooms. "What happened?"

"That's complicated. There's what I thought happened. And then what we only recently found out was the truth." She paused to make another cracker and chase it with wine. Grey gave her the space to gather her thoughts.

"When Jonah was eight and Sam was five, Lonnie walked

out on all of us. No explanation. No question. No fighting. He just walked away from our entire family and asked for a divorce. And after that divorce, he didn't want anything to do with the kids or me. Waived his parental rights. He was the one who asked for the name change. The kids don't know that part. But I saw it for what it was. Another way to cut us off."

Grey's hand fisted on the hilt of the knife. This didn't sound at all like the man he'd known. The man he'd once considered a brother. "That must have been devastating."

"Yeah. I mean, it would have been one thing if we'd been fighting and having problems. But this just came entirely out of left field. For a long time, I wondered if he'd met someone else. If he regretted marrying so young and starting a family immediately." She took a bigger swig of wine. "As far as I'm aware, he never had any prolonged relationship with anyone. He just chose to be alone. Like he'd hit his quota and maxed out on what he was willing to endure for family." Something raw and ragged passed over her face.

Grey laid his hand over hers, wanting to offer comfort. "I'm sorry." Family had always been at the center of what she'd wanted, so he couldn't imagine how deeply that had cut her.

She turned her hand up to link with his and squeezed, offering a sad smile. "That was what we believed for years. Then he died, and because of a lot of complicated stuff I really don't want to get into tonight, we found out that he'd basically been blackmailed."

Whatever explanations Grey might have imagined, that hadn't even made the list. "Blackmailed. To leave you?"

"Not directly. Long story very short, he got involved in something he shouldn't have. When he tried to get out, they threatened us as his family."

"Why the hell didn't y'all just leave town? Or go to the police?"

With a helpless shrug, she pulled away. "I never knew about

any of this when it was happening. I don't know why Lonnie chose the nuclear option. I don't know why he didn't feel like he could talk to me. I guess he thought there was no hope of escape from his poor choices, and no circumstance where he got to keep the life we'd built." She turned the wineglass between her fingers, her gaze going unfocused.

Did she miss that life? Was she grieving the loss of it all over again? Somewhere under all the hurt she'd lived with, did she still love Lonnie?

Grey didn't know how to ask, and either way, Lonnie was dead.

Seeming to come back to herself, Rebecca took another sip of wine. "The kids are still struggling to reconcile everything we found out. Sam was young enough when he left that she doesn't have a lot of the good memories. But Jonah remembers, and he felt so much more betrayal. I think it was worst on him. He stopped being a child that day. My sweet, fun, funny little boy decided he had to be a man because Lonnie wouldn't be. And I'm so damned proud of who he's become, but I hate what he had to go through to get there."

"What about you?" No way had she come out of that shit unscathed.

"I'm still wrestling with my own feelings over the whole thing. Because I lived with decades of believing the worst of Lonnie. Of trying to reconcile the man he'd become with the one that I married. The one who'd been my friend since the second grade. Only to find out that he wasn't the terrible person I imagined him to be. God knows, he wasn't perfect. But I think, in the end, his heart was in the right place. That helps. But I don't think I can ever forgive him for robbing my son of his childhood, no matter what his reasons."

The man she'd married, not the man she loved. Was that significant? Or was it just where she'd landed after all those years of living with a twisted truth? And did she even realize she'd called Jonah her son, not *their* son? Did that mean something? Had she effectively cut Lonnie off as a parent in her own mind when he'd walked away? Or was there something else there?

Maybe Grey was simply looking for confirmation of what he wanted to be true.

Either way, there was no escaping the fact that Lonnie had been weak. Whatever he'd been into, there were a thousand other ways he could've handled the situation. But instead, he'd chosen to walk away. To be alone instead of finding a way to make things right with his family. None of that was what Grey had imagined when he'd found out his best friend had married Rebecca. And it sure as shit wasn't what she'd deserved.

If he'd known...

But he hadn't known, because he'd devoted himself to the career he'd chosen over her, and he hadn't let himself look back. Even when confronted with Jonah and the knowledge that Rebecca was divorced, he hadn't come back to check on her. Not until now.

A potent cocktail of regret churned in his gut. So many what ifs. So many lost years.

Grey scrubbed a hand over his face and braced himself against the counter. "You looked so damned happy in the beginning. It was the only reason I could keep away from you. Because I told myself I didn't have the right to fuck that up for you."

Eyes wide, Rebecca slowly set her wineglass on the counter. "What are you talking about?"

He forced himself to meet her gaze. "I came back in May. After exams. Before I left for my summer rotation with ROTC."

"What? But I never..."

"Never saw me. No. I saw you with Lonnie. You were pregnant. Had his ring on your finger." And God, that had cut him

off at the knees. Was there any more obvious sign that she
belonged to another man?

All color had leeched from her face. "Why didn't you say
something?"

He mustered up a smile he knew didn't reach his eyes. "As
far as I could tell, you were happy. You'd gotten what you wanted." She'd leapt feet-first into that quiet, small-town life with
somebody who wanted the same. "Who was I to stand in the
way of that?"

Her face twisted with some expression he couldn't read. Her
throat worked. "I thought the same of you and the Navy." She
paused, eyes glimmering with tears. "Did you find what you
were looking for out there?"

"Some of it. I had a good career."

"No family?"

Grey shook his head. "Never married."

"Never found the right woman?"

"The right woman didn't want to share me with the Navy."

"The right woman didn't want to share me with the Navy."

The statement hit Rebecca like a mortar round because he
simply stood there, hands braced on the counter, gaze steady
on hers, utterly self-possessed.

He'd come back. Exactly as he'd said he would. And she'd
never known. She had no idea what might have changed if she
had, because she'd already married Lonnie by then. But there
was no stopping the tidal wave of regret and longing. Because
he was right. She'd never wanted to share him with the Navy.
And in her selfishness, she'd hurt him for even thinking
she'd try.

She'd spent plenty of years hating herself for that. For the
immaturity and the weakness that meant she couldn't trust him

when it had mattered most. For the fear that had changed both their lives. But never more than this moment, when she faced the outright proof that what he'd felt for her hadn't changed. Because he'd always been everything she wanted, and she'd wasted so many years alone.

Swallowing against the burn of tears, she gathered together whatever scraps of poise she could manage. "The Universe has a funny way of teaching you lessons. I was so hard on you. And then I had to face the whole thing all over again with my son when he declared he wanted to be a SEAL. I didn't want to lose him, too, so I had to let him go and trust that he'd come home. And that was even worse than watching you walk away, because that's my baby. I rocked him to sleep and kissed his booboos and bandaged his skinned knees. But I saw what it meant to him to do it. To pursue that bigger purpose. To be that kind of man. And I finally understood, at least a little, why you had to go. And when I did—" She shook her head. "I've thought about that night so often and with so much regret."

"You wanted a different kind of life." He said it easily, as if stating an oft-repeated fact.

But she could see the hints of old pain beneath and wanted to give him what honesty she could. "I wanted you. And I didn't trust that you'd come back to me if you left. It's a big, wide world out there, and I thought that if you got a taste of it, I wouldn't be enough for you."

He was around the counter before she could blink, stopping just inches away, his chest heaving. "No. No, that's never been true."

She looked up into his face, seeing everything she'd convinced herself she'd imagined at eighteen. She wanted to cheer. To weep. To touch him. For him to touch her.

As if reading her mind, he skimmed his fingers over her cheek, and she couldn't stop herself from turning into the caress, chasing the warmth. His callused palm cupped her face, and everything inside her began to quake. It was too much sensation and not nearly enough.

"Grey." His name came out as a sigh. A question.

In answer, he bent to take her mouth.

That first touch of his lips on hers was an earthquake. Shocking and foundation shaking. It had been an eon since she'd felt the intimacy of a kiss. An eternity since anything more. All those sensations, all those needs and wants, had gone dormant, been forgotten. But that gentle brush of contact brought all of it roaring back to life. Every sip told her she mattered. Every sigh stripped away another layer of the old anxiety that had cloaked her like varnish for years.

There was no demand. No domination or conquering. He *gave*. Comfort. Tenderness. Apology. And like a moth to a flame, she flew toward it all, sliding off the stool to wrap around him. He pulled her close, anchoring her against that hard body that was bigger and taller than she remembered, and yet still somehow felt familiar. He angled his head, sliding them both deeper into desire. Her heart thundered in her chest, chanting *yes, yes, yes*. But something else, something deeper, had tendrils of panic licking through her.

Grey eased back, pressing his brow to hers, his strong, capable hand cupping her nape. "You're shaking."

"I know." Because he felt like the only stable thing in her orbit, she clung to him, breathing the air he breathed, soaking in his nearness as she struggled to find some kind of even footing.

He made no effort to move away, just held her for long minutes, stroking her back until the trembling finally abated. Even then, he didn't let her go, just brushed the hair back from her face. "Better?"

She looked into those hazel eyes, noting the lines at the corners. "Steadier, anyway."

"I should feed you." But still, he didn't release her or step back. He seemed to be waiting for something.

An explanation? How could she explain something she barely understood herself? He'd crashed back into her world after all these years and shattered all the assumptions she'd based her life on.

Her fingers flexed against his back, betraying the compulsion to latch on and never let go again. "I wasn't expecting this. I wasn't expecting you. Not after how we left things."

"I stopped holding a grudge a long time ago. But I'd be lying if I didn't admit you were a big part of what brought me home." His fingers skimmed her cheek again as he tucked her hair behind her ear. "It's still here, Rebel. And it's only fair I warn you, I intend to follow up on that, unless you tell me right here, right now, that you're not interested. If you're not, that's your right. We'll have a nice meal, and I'll take you home, and we'll let the past be the past. But if you are..." He trailed off, letting her fill in the blanks.

She hadn't pursued anyone after her divorce. All her bandwidth had gone into her business and making sure her children were taken care of. There'd been none left over to put toward someone else, and no one who'd ever tempted her to try. And even when the kids were grown, off living their own lives, she hadn't bothered. There'd been a part of her that hadn't been able to trust her own judgment, assuming she had lousy taste in men. But it had never been that. It was that no one else was him. She'd spent more than thirty years using him as the yardstick and finding every other man falling short.

Her skin was on fire where he'd touched her, and the heart she'd tried to numb so long ago thumped with longing and anticipation. This was a second chance. One she never imagined they'd get. One she didn't want to walk away from, no matter how hard, how difficult this road was going to be.

"I can't tell you I'm not interested."

His mouth curved into a satisfied smile that warmed his eyes. "Good."

When he started to step back, she tightened her hold for just a moment. "Grey, I need to tell you—" God, *how* did she say it?

He smiled, framing her face. "We can take this at whatever pace you want, so long as we both get to the same place in the end."

He thought this was about her being gun-shy. And, well, maybe she was. But not for any of the reasons he might've imagined. But right now, she wanted to take him at his word. That they wanted to get to the same place. The same page. Something they hadn't managed at eighteen. Had maybe not been capable of back then. "I'd like that. I'd like that very much."

This time, when he stepped back, she let him go.

"Then for tonight, let's put the past way. I want to wow you with my culinary accomplishments and talk about the future. And at midnight, I want to kiss you again, to ring in the New Year."

"That sounds like a pretty amazing end to the year."

He lifted one of her hands to his lips. "Tonight is only the beginning."

Giving in to the charm and delight, Rebecca let go of the worry for the moment and grinned. "You definitely have more game than you had at eighteen."

"I look forward to showing it off."

As he moved back around the counter to resume his abandoned meal prep, she settled back onto her stool and poured another glass of wine. This was worth it. He was worth it.

But how the hell was she going to tell him he had a son?

4

Grey was whistling as he pulled open the door to Bradford Realty. And why shouldn't he be? His New Year's Eve date with Rebel had gone better than he'd anticipated, with hours of conversation that proved they still enjoyed each other's company, and a goodnight kiss that had curled both their toes. If he'd been a little disappointed she hadn't invited him in, he was only human. But he'd meant what he'd told her. He didn't care what pace they took, so long as they got to the same destination. She was worth every second of waiting. At this age, they both had baggage, and given how her marriage had turned out, she was bound to be a little wary. It was enough that she wanted this second chance, too.

A young woman in a chunky maroon sweater and skinny jeans looked up from the front desk. "Welcome to Bradford Realty. How can we help you?"

"I'd like to talk to someone about some property. I'm looking to relocate to the area."

"Of course, we can help you with that. One moment." The brunette picked up a phone and pressed a button for some internal line. "Are you available for a walk-in? Great. Be back in a minute." She hung up and rose with a smile. "Right this way."

Grey followed her down a short hall and, at her invitation, stepped into an office.

The woman behind the desk hefted herself up, leading with an enormous baby belly.

Grey took two steps forward. "Oh please, don't get up. I... uh."

Having achieved her feet, the woman laughed, her teeth flashing stark white against flawless reddish-brown skin. "I can assure you that, contrary to all appearances, I'm not due for another month, at least." He must've still looked panicked as he shook her hand because she winked at him. "Promise. My first was a whole two weeks past his due date. I'm Magnolia Bradford. What can I do for you, Captain Greyson?"

Grey blinked, pausing with his ass halfway to the seat of a chair. "I'm sorry. Have we met?"

That smile flashed again, showing dimples in her round cheeks. "No, but you've made a bit of an impression since you hit town, and everybody's talking about you going out with Rebecca Ferguson."

How had he forgotten that this was what small towns were like? It wasn't as if the military didn't have its own chains of gossip, but this was different. Grey didn't know what to do with the fact that people were talking about him and Rebecca. He didn't mind it, but even he recognized that if he confirmed the rumor and it got back to Jonah before one of them talked to him about them, it could be problematic.

"We're old friends." It wasn't really a confirmation or denial. It was simply a truth. Wanting to get on down to business, he settled in his chair. "I'm in the market for property."

"Well, you've come to the right place." Magnolia tugged over a legal pad. "What are you looking for?"

He'd been giving a lot of thought to this as he'd worked on

his business plan. "I need acreage. Minimum of a hundred, but preferably more, with varied terrain. Mountains, woods, open spaces. A water source, if possible. A creek or lake. I'd prefer something that already has a house or cabin or some form of dwelling already on it. I'm not fussy about what because ultimately, I'll likely build my own house, but I'd like somewhere to live on property while that's being done."

He considered going into more detail about what he wanted to do, but that seemed like too much at this point, and anyway, he wanted to tell Rebecca first. They hadn't gotten around to that on their date the other night, and she'd had plans with friends for New Year's Day. He was itching to see her again. To taste her again.

"What's your budget?" Magnolia's voice brought him back to the current conversation.

Grey named a figure that had her neat brows arching.

"Okay. How far afield are we looking?"

That was certainly a question. He didn't want to get too far from Rebel, but he was also aware that, to do what he wanted to do, he might have to make some compromises. "I'd prefer something that's localish. This county or one adjacent. But go as far as you have to. I realize it's an unusual request and might take some time to find the right fit."

"I'll start looking and hopefully have some properties to show you in a day or two. I have a few ideas, but I want to chase down the particulars. How long are you in town?"

"For the foreseeable future. I've rented a place."

She wrote down his contact information. "I'll be in touch as soon as I've got something to show you."

"Great. I look forward to working with you." He rose and extended his hand across the desk before she could try to stand again. "Please. Keep your seat. I'll see myself out."

Her chortling laugh followed him down the hall.

Did all men feel this vague sense of alarm being around a

very pregnant woman? Or was it just him because he hadn't done it very often? Having never married, he hadn't had a family of his own. Hadn't had a front-row seat to the whole miraculous process of growing a human. Honestly, since he'd seen a very pregnant Rebecca all those years ago, he'd made a not-so-subtle effort to steer clear of expecting women. It brought up too many memories, too much longing he couldn't do anything about. But he found himself wondering about it now. About what pregnancy had been like for her. About what kind of partner he'd have been.

An absentee one, most likely, given how his career had gone. Even if he hadn't chosen the SEALS, the military wasn't designed for traditional family life, and all too often, fathers missed the whole process of pregnancy and birth. Grey wouldn't have wanted that for her. Wouldn't have wanted that for a child. So many servicemen went home to strained and part-time relationships with their kids, wanting to be a part of their lives while they could be and not always finding a way to fit. They were strangers to their own families. Some managed it better than others, but it was a hard life for a family. Not everybody was made to handle it. So, as awful as it had been, maybe she'd made the right call, putting her foot down and not being willing to compromise.

With Rebel on his mind, his feet carried him down the sidewalk, through the streets of downtown. City workers with ladders were taking down the garland and lights that had lent a festive air for the holidays. It was officially a new year. The air was brisk and the day beautiful. Content to walk, Grey soaked in the changes. Eden's Ridge had grown in the past thirty years. The downtown that had once taken up only two blocks along Main Street, now stretched for nearly four, with businesses fanning out along adjacent side streets. Though things were fairly sleepy now, there were signs of tourism. A spiffing up that had visited all the shopfronts, and a handful of businesses that went along with the tourist trade. He passed more than one storefront with papered windows hiding internal renovations. More new businesses coming to town. The signs of growth were good. Far too many small towns struggled these days.

He spotted Rebecca through the shop window, her head thrown back in a laugh. God, he'd missed that laugh. Tugging open the door, he stepped inside.

She swung toward him, and that fading laugh turned into a megawatt smile that punched him in the chest and left him feeling more than a little emotionally drunk.

"Hey, you. I wasn't expecting to see you this morning."

Because he wanted to grab her and kiss her, he shoved both hands into his pockets. "I had business downtown. And I realized that I still forgot to get your number."

"Well, pull out your phone."

Aware of the curious gazes of the half-dozen women in the shop, in the midst of various beauty treatments, Grey kept his attention on her as he opened a new contact and entered her name. "Go ahead."

She reeled off her number.

As soon as he had it saved, he toggled over to send her a text message.

Grey: *I want to see you again.*

Somewhere, a phone dinged.

"There. Now you've got mine, too." Shoving his phone into his pocket, he backed toward the door. "I know you're working. I'll get out of your hair. See you later, Rebel."

"Bye."

He hadn't made it five feet out the door before his phone vibrated with a text. Fishing it out, he read her reply.

A GIF of Bill Murray from *Groundhog Day* saying "Me, also," followed by *How about tonight? Dinner at my house.*

Not bothering to hold in the grin, he thumbed a message back.

That sounds perfect.
Rebecca: *See you at seven.*
Whistling again, he headed back for his SUV.

REBECCA HAD DELIBERATELY SET her dinner with Grey later to
give herself time to swing by Garden of Eden to grab ingredients for what she knew had been one of his favorite meals.
She'd had every intention of getting the house picked up and
presentable for company again. There was even supposed to be
time to shave. Not that she was necessarily planning to go to
bed with him tonight, but it never hurt to be prepared.

What she had not been prepared for was Otis.

Jonah and Rachel had elected to adopt the puppy a few
months before. He was a mix of labrador and something huge,
with paws that suggested he might rival her for size once he was
full grown. He'd hit that gangly stage of puppyhood, where he
stumbled all over his feet and into things. All the puppy play-
fulness in a body he didn't realize was forty pounds and growing. Rebecca had volunteered to keep him while the kids were
in New York, a decision she was regretting as the little trouble-
maker evaded her again, her best bra clamped between his
teeth. He'd swiped it out of her underwear drawer as she'd been
getting ready. That thing was La Perla, damn it. Blue silk with
frastaglio lace, she'd bought it on sale on her fiftieth birthday, to
remind herself she wasn't old, and she'd only worn it a handful
of times. She damned well wasn't giving up without a fight.

"Otis, you drop that right now!"

Eyes bright with glee over the game he thought they were
playing, the puppy scrambled onto the sofa, leaping over the
arm and racing toward the kitchen.

"Oh, for the love of—"

The doorbell rang.

Crap! She hadn't gotten dinner started, hadn't gotten her bath, hadn't even changed clothes yet. And he was *here*.

"You are not even on the list of my favorite grandchildren, dog!"

Abandoning pursuit of the thief, Rebecca sucked in a few breaths and tried to calm herself. It was fine. This was Grey. The guy who'd been there for her entire awkward tween years. He could handle seeing her in the same jeans and sweater she'd worn to work.

She pulled open the door to find a big bouquet of irises in her field of view. "Oh." Her temper immediately softened.

Grey peered around the flowers, arching a brow. "You okay? You're out of breath."

"I've been having a standoff with the dog. He thinks we're playing keep away."

He looked confused. "You have a dog?"

"Jonah and Rachel have a dog. I'm dog-sitting until they're back from Syracuse tomorrow, so I'm a little behind on everything. Come on in."

Lured by the prospect of someone new to adore him, Otis came prancing to the door, the bra dangling from his mouth, his tail whirling like a helicopter.

Grey pointed at the puppy. "Drop it!"

At the unmistakable command in the tone, Otis plopped his butt to the floor and opened his mouth.

Too stunned by her own heated reaction to that voice, Rebecca wasn't fast enough to snatch the bra from where it landed at Grey's feet. He shifted the flowers to the crook of his arm and crouched, scratching the dog's head with one hand and picking up the lingerie with the other. By the time he straightened to his full height, his eyes had turned molten.

"I... um." Jesus, she couldn't think with him looking at her like that. As if he really hoped she'd put it on so he could take it right back off again. With his teeth.

Oh, mercy.

Without a word, he held out the bra.

Pressing her lips together, she gingerly took it. "I'll be right back."

Face flaming, she hurried down the hall to her room, stowing the bra in the closet. She'd examine the damage later.

Shutting the door behind her, she rejoined Grey in the living room. He was still smoldering at her as he extended the flowers. "These are for you."

More than a little fluttery, she took the bouquet. The combination of the smolder and the sweetness made her a little light-headed. No one had given her flowers in a romantic context... well... ever. Lonnie had been more apt to surprise her with her favorite candy or bring something home for the kids. No one had ever tried to romance her before. Not really.

Riding the wave of gratitude and pleasure, she rose to her toes, sliding her free arm up his chest to tug his mouth down to hers. She meant it to be soft and sweet. And brief. But his arms came around her, banding her against the strength of his body. Moaning with approval, she pressed closer, ready and willing as he took the kiss deeper, until she wanted to forget all about the flowers and dinner and drag him straight back to her room for an entirely different kind of dessert than the pie she had planned.

Otis barked, reminding her of the forty-five-minute game of keep away and the fact that she hadn't shaved.

Damn it. Maybe he wouldn't care, but by God, she wasn't breaking her celibacy with hairy legs.

Struggling to find some control, she throttled back the kiss, dropping to her feet. "Well, it's a good thing I didn't have time to redo my makeup."

"Not like you need it."

Huffing a laugh, she eased out of his hold. "Thanks for that. And for the flowers. They're gorgeous."

He trailed her into the kitchen, watching as she found a vase and put the irises in water. They made a lovely centerpiece to the kitchen table, and she automatically pulled out placemats, napkins, and candles to make a little tablescape.

"Dinner will be a little late. Courtesy of the mischief maker over there, I haven't gotten it started yet."

"I'm sure we can find a way to entertain ourselves."

Did he *mean* for his voice to sound like pure sex? Or was that just her long-neglected libido panting after him?

Squeezing her thighs together, she took a few more calming breaths and moved to the sink to wash her hands. "Let me just get this started."

"Want me to play sous chef?"

"If you like."

He moved beside her at the sink, close enough his shoulder brushed hers as he thrust his hands beneath the running water. Needing some distance to keep her head, she dried off her hands and began pulling out ingredients.

"What can I do?"

"Debone that rotisserie chicken while I get the pasta started."

Quickly rolling up the sleeves of his black button-down shirt, he opened the deli container and began pulling meat off the bone. Meanwhile, she started a large pot of water for pasta and set the oven to preheat. When she began piling assorted cans of soup, sour cream, cream cheese, butter, and spices on the counter, his eyes brightened. "Are you making chicken tetrazzini?"

"Yeah. It's your mom's recipe."

Grey sucked in a breath, and she was afraid she'd made a misstep. His voice, when he spoke, was a little thicker. "I haven't had it since she died. Damn, I've missed it."

Heart recognizing the ache of loss, she stroked a hand down his arm. "When did you lose her?"

"Last year. Cancer." Twitching his shoulders, he got back to work on the chicken. "Dad passed about five years ago. Stroke in his sleep."

"I'm sorry. I know what it's like." She began mixing ingredients for the casserole. "Daddy had a heart attack when the kids were in college. Mama wasn't ever really the same after that. She wasn't sick. The doctor said she was in remarkably good health. One day she just... didn't wake up. I think she just didn't want to go on without him."

"From what I remember, your parents were devoted to each other."

Rebecca smiled, remembering. "They were. I think that's part of why I never dated after my divorce. If I couldn't have what they had, I didn't want to make the effort."

His hands stilled. "You haven't dated? At all?"

She refused to be embarrassed about that. "No." When he only continued to stare, she arched a brow in challenge. "That shocks you."

"Yeah. I mean, you're a vibrant, beautiful woman. I'd have thought you'd want companionship, at the least."

"I figured out a long time ago that what I want and what I need are often not the same thing. I learned how to do without a lot. But since Lonnie died, I guess I've been rethinking everything. He was our age. Not a spring chicken, but not old. It's sobering to know that it can all be snuffed out in an instant. I feel fortunate to still be here. To see my kids marry and start their own families. I certainly hope I've got a lot of years to go, but you never know. And I find that I don't want to waste whatever time I have left. I don't want to have more regrets when I'm called home."

"Do you have a lot of regrets?"

"When it comes to you? So many."

Her gaze snagged on his and held. It was so damned hard not to get trapped in all the what ifs. Those of the past. Those of the present. Yet if she let herself fall down that rabbit hole, she'd paralyze herself with indecision.

The pasta on the stove boiled over, breaking the tension. She spun toward it, nudging the pot off the heat and quickly sopping up water from the stovetop with a kitchen towel.

"For what it's worth, not coming back sooner was the biggest of mine."

Clutching the towel, she turned to face him. "You came back. That's what matters."

Clearly tired of being ignored, Otis gave a yowling bark and started to jump up toward the chicken.

Grey twisted, neatly blocking the jump with a knee. "No, sir. Down."

The puppy talked back, as if to say, "But, chicken!"

"Do I look like I have 'Sucker' tattooed on my forehead?"

Otis laid down, head on his paws, face mournful.

Rebecca laughed, glad for the clear change of mood. "So, what was your business downtown today?"

He handed over the chicken for her to add to the casserole. "I was meeting with a realtor."

"Oh, you're buying a house?"

"Well, I'm looking to buy land. Hopefully, there will be some kind of dwelling on it to start until I can build what I want. But no, I plan to open a center to help aid in the transition period for veterans moving back into civilian society."

"Like the program Jonah did?"

"Less skills training and more helping vets find their new purpose. I did something similar out in Montana when I got out."

By the time she'd assembled the casserole, he'd given her the overview. It was an ambitious project. Then again, he'd always been an ambitious man.

"Do you think you'll really be able to do that here?"

"I'm trying to find a property so that I can do that here."

She slid the casserole into the oven and set the timer on autopilot.

Would he find what he actually needed here? If he didn't, did that mean he was leaving again? Just the idea of it had her gut twisting into knots. She couldn't voice the worry. Her not being able to trust him in the first place had led to so many problems. She could wait and see.

Grey was right there as she straightened. He took her hands in his. "Look, it's one idea for what I can do with my retirement. It's not the only thing. It's just what I'm exploring right now. If it doesn't work out, then it doesn't work out, and I'll come up with something else. I'm not going anywhere. Not so long as you're here. Okay?"

Looking into his face, she believed him. The tension bled out. "Okay."

He brushed a kiss to her brow. "Good. Because we've got a bigger thing to figure out."

"What's that?"

"How are we going to tell Jonah we're dating?"

5

Grey pulled into the parking lot of Bad Boy Bakers at a quarter to ten. He'd estimated this ought to be past the breakfast rush and before the crowds started for the daily lunch special. After much discussion, he and Rebecca had decided this news would be marginally better coming from him, as Jonah would likely appreciate the man-to-man discussion. Grey wasn't actually sure that was true, but better Jonah's displeasure come at him than at her. He wanted a chance to set the boy straight, if necessary.

The bell rang, announcing his entrance. Jonah was at the register, checking out a customer. His friendly smile didn't waver as he continued the transaction, but he exchanged a look with Brax, who nodded once and strode out from behind the counter. Grey watched as he went to the window and turned the sign to *Closed*. The display cases were still half full. Holt emerged from the kitchen, shooting Grey a steely stare as he helped process the last two customers.

They knew.

Not the way Grey had wanted things to go, but he'd deal

with the situation one way or the other. Aware this might turn more antagonistic than he'd planned, he stood back, waiting as Jonah escorted those remaining customers to the door. Someone else was about to come in.

He flashed an apologetic smile at the woman. "I'm sorry, we've got to close for just a bit. We'll be open again in fifteen minutes." Then he shut the door in her face. The moment the lock clicked, his amiable expression faded, and it was clear he was pissed. That temper was leashed, but he definitely wasn't happy.

Grey had expected this. "Who told you?"

At Jonah's sides, his hands flexed and released. "At least five people. What the hell are you doing with my mother?"

This was coming from a place of protection. Jonah had been the man in Rebecca's life from the time he was eight years old. And she had two more protectors in the honorary sons who came to flank him. Grey appreciated them looking out for her and respected the love they clearly had for her. Because of that, he didn't brook offense when they all crossed their arms, bowing up in some kind of intimidation tactic.

"What I'm doing is courting her."

Jonah blinked at the old-fashioned term. Given how things were going, it was entirely probable they'd blow on past that stage pretty quickly, but Grey wanted to romance her in a way he hadn't been able to back in the day, so the phrase still applied.

"You're... what?"

"Are you aware that your mom is a brilliant, beautiful, vibrant woman in the prime of her life?"

"My mom is awesome. I'm aware. What does that have to do with anything?"

Did the kid even hear himself? "Everything. Look, I care about your mother. I cared about her well before you were born. She was one of my best friends growing up, and we have a shared history that you know very little about. We have a connection that we've mutually chosen to explore. I came here today to tell you about it, out of respect for you and the relationship that you and I have had. But understand this: I'm not here for your permission. I don't need it, and neither does she."

A muscle ticked in the younger man's jaw. Oh yeah, he didn't like that.

"I appreciate that all y'all want to look out for her. You're her son. Y'all are her unofficial sons. Those protective instincts speak well of all of you. But don't interfere. That's just gonna piss us both off. I know your mom hasn't been seeing anybody —" a fact which still blew Grey's mind, "—so you haven't really had to do this before, but she's a grown adult and can make her own decisions. Right now, that decision is to see me."

The silent standoff continued for another long minute. Grey said nothing, letting Jonah do whatever he needed to do to swallow down the anger and frustration.

"I won't see her hurt. Not again."

Shoving down his instinctive insult at the implication, Grey folded his own arms. "Are you under the impression that your mother is fragile? Because I can assure you that the strength and tenacity that carried you through BUDS and completing countless missions as a SEAL sure as hell didn't come from Lonnie."

Jonah's brows slammed together. "I thought you were friends."

"We were. That doesn't mean I was blind to his faults." He dared a step closer. "I know you've got complicated feelings about him, but I'm not him. The last thing in the world I want to do is hurt Rebecca. I know what she's been through. She deserved a hell of a lot better, and I intend to give it to her."

"That sounds pretty damned declarative," Brax observed.

"I'm not operating on maybes. Not with her. I'm around as long as she'll have me. Can I promise I won't fuck it up? No. I've got a Y chromosome, so that pretty much guarantees I'll screw something up. But I give you my word I'll do my best not to, and own up to my mistakes when I make them. I'll treat her with respect and friendship." *And love.*

But he didn't mention that to her son, because it was clear the kid was struggling more than a little with the whole thing, and it hardly made sense to tell him when he hadn't outright admitted it to Rebel yet. He didn't want to scare her off by pushing too hard, too fast.

"I don't like it."

"You don't have to like it. You just have to respect it. Let me ask you something: Would you have a problem with any guy dating your mother? Or is it specifically me, because of who I am to you?"

Jonah's gaze shot up, his shoulders dropping in surprise at the question. "It's..." He seemed to flail around for the right word. "Weird."

Grey bit back a smile. "Weird how?"

"You're part of a different life. I don't know how to wrap my brain around you being in this one. And being in this one connected to her instead of me."

For the first time, it occurred to him that maybe some of Jonah's inflexibility about this wasn't about his mom.

"My history with her doesn't negate my history with you. All those years we worked together, served together, haven't just gone away. And I hope you don't want to dissolve that association just because there's an extra layer of connection between us than there was before."

Possibly more of a connection than Jonah could imagine. But those suspicions were a long way from being confirmed, and Grey wasn't about to screw up his second chance with Rebecca by bringing it up before she was ready.

Jonah's shoulders relaxed. "No, sir. I don't want that. I just want her to be happy."

"So do I. We both realize there's gonna be an adjustment period for all this. Maybe in the meantime, you could work on calling me Grey?"

His face flexed. "I think I'm gonna have to work up to it. I've got a lot of years of military protocol to overcome."

Grey chuckled. "Fair enough. Are we okay?"

"As long as you treat her right... yeah."

That was good enough for him.

"Girl, when you break a streak, you go *big!*" From her seat in Rebecca's stylist chair, Crystal Blue closed her eyes and shimmied her shoulders. "Mmm mmm mmm. That man is H-O-T hot."

Rebecca's cheeks heated. As Crystal owned the local diner, if it wasn't already all over town that she and Grey were dating, it would be by the end of the day. And that was... fine. She didn't love being the center of gossip—she much preferred dishing it—but it wasn't her first time in the spotlight. After Lonnie left her, she'd been the subject of all kinds of speculation for years. At least this go round, it wasn't negative attention.

She just hoped Grey got to Jonah before the gossip train did. That wasn't how her son needed to hear about this. She still wasn't entirely sure this was best coming from Grey. If he'd been anyone else, there'd have been no question. But given the two of them already had a prior relationship, maybe he had a point. God knew, things would be tough enough when the truth came out. She didn't want anything else to damage that foundation.

"If I'd known you had that to wait on, I wouldn't have ragged on your single status so long," Candice interjected.

"I wasn't waiting for him." The idea that she'd been actively delaying her life somehow, because of a man, stuck in Rebecca's craw. "I had no idea he was planning on coming back to Eden's Ridge."

Donna, ever the peacemaker, simply smiled from Candice's chair. "Well, whether you knew or not, obviously he's something special to have overcome your self-imposed ban on dating."

Resuming the application of color to the rest of Crystal's hair, Rebecca made a half-hearted protest. "It wasn't a ban exactly. There was just nobody who seemed worth the effort."

"That one looks worth all kinds of effort," Crystal declared. "Worth trying out that new gym they put in around the block."

With a bland stare, she worked the color through with gloved fingers. "I hardly think a new training program at a gym is going to make up for thirty years and birthing two kids."

She'd very deliberately avoided thinking about how different her body was now than it had been the last time Grey had seen her naked. Back then, she'd been young, fit, and pageant-ready. She'd spent most of her adult life unlearning disordered behavior and thoughts around eating and health, and she wasn't undoing all that hard work over any man. Not even Grey. If he had an issue with her older body, then he wasn't the guy for her. End of story. But given their chemistry was still alive and well, she didn't think he'd suddenly be repulsed by a little extra padding and skin that wasn't quite as firm as it used to be.

"Oh, whatever. You're gorgeous exactly as you are," Candice put in. "But maybe you should step up your cardio. You know... up your endurance. Just in case." She added an eyebrow waggle and a grin, in case anyone missed her meaning.

She was not going to stand here and imagine acrobatic sex with Grey. She was *not*.

"Remind me why we're friends?" As her business partner laughed, Rebecca lifted the bowl and brush. "I'm gonna go rinse these out." And if she happened to put a cold cloth on the back of her neck and her face while she was back there, nobody would be able to see.

Why hadn't he texted? Was he still at the bakery? Had Jonah taken it badly? Grey had mentioned he had an appointment after to go check out some property with Magnolia, so maybe he simply hadn't had a chance to send the update. She'd get through this cut and color, and if he hadn't messaged her by then, she'd text him.

Hearing the shop bell tinkle, Rebecca dumped the bowl in the sink, stripped off her gloves, and hurried out, thinking maybe Grey had stopped by in person to let her know how it went. But it was her son who stood in the entry, hands shoved into his pockets, his shoulders stiff.

"Jonah! How was your trip to New York?" Candice sang out.

"It was good."

"Did things go well with your future in-laws?" Donna asked.

"Yep. They're nice folks."

He wasn't even making a pretense of sociability. He'd definitely been told, and it was equally obvious he wasn't exactly happy about the whole thing.

Not wanting this conversation to be fodder for the grapevine, she set a timer on her watch. "I'll be back in just a bit. Candice, in case I get delayed, Crystal's got about half an hour left on that color."

"No problem."

She snagged her coat and pushed out of the shop, trusting Jonah would follow.

After a brief, "Ladies," acknowledging the group, he joined her out on the sidewalk.

"Why don't we walk a bit?" It would give them a modicum of privacy and keep her from wringing her hands in anxiety.

"Sure." Jonah fell into step beside her.

After waiting an endless minute to see if he'd start, Rebecca took the leap herself. "I'm sure you have questions."

"Really, only one. Why him? All these years, there's been nobody. Or at least nobody I knew about. So why did you have to pick my former CO?"

That hadn't been the question she'd expected from him, but given his relationship with Grey, it made sense.

"It has nothing to do with him being your CO. It's because he's a good man." *And you're just like him.* The more time she spent with Grey, the more evidence she had that Jonah was just like his father. But she was hardly going to bring that up on the street. "And because now is the time we have. We had feelings for each other a long time ago, and we didn't work out at the time because we were on different life paths. Now those paths have crossed again, and we want to give it another shot."

At the mention of feelings, his shoulders hunched up toward his ears. "So you really have a... thing for him?"

Rebecca huffed a laugh. "Yes, I really have a thing for him. Is that so hard to believe?"

"Yes. No. I don't know. It feels fast."

"Baby, we're dating, not running off to elope in Vegas."

He shot her a sidelong look. "I mean... Sam and Griff did it. Twice."

"So they did," she conceded. "Look, Grey and I have a history, and we're attracted to each other."

Because he looked a little green, she had to press him. "Honey, would you honestly rather I be alone for the rest of my life, just to make you more comfortable?"

His eyes widened, and color crept up his throat. "No. It's just weird. I'm gonna have to get used to it."

You're going to have to get used to a whole lot more than that.

It wasn't the first time she'd considered how Jonah would react if he found out that Lonnie wasn't his father. But it was the first time she'd thought about it since the possibility of him finding out had become a probability, and one that would happen sooner rather than later. She truly had no idea how he'd respond. He had immense respect for Grey as a commanding officer. She knew his feelings about Lonnie were complicated, all wrapped up in what he'd believed all his life, only recently colored by the truth that had come out a few months ago. But to find out that his father was someone else entirely—someone who was, by all Jonah's measures, a better man—well, she hoped he'd take some comfort in that.

But she knew he'd be upset at the deception, regardless of her reasons, and she hadn't figured out exactly how to deal with that. She didn't know how to explain to either of them that the choices she'd made at eighteen weren't the ones she'd make now. Could either of them remember being that young? Enough to cut her some slack for acting out of fear?

Grey had to come first in this. She'd been telling herself she needed to get them on a more solid foundation, to clearly understand who he was now and where he stood in order to determine the right way to break the news to him. There really was no truly good way, but there were a lot of bad ones, and she wanted to avoid as many of those as possible. If a tiny voice in the back of her head told her she was just being chicken about the whole thing by putting it off, she dismissed it. This was the smart play for now.

As they turned the last corner to make the block, Jonah took her arm and shifted to face her. "I just want you to be happy, Mom. You deserve that. If he makes you happy, then I'll get okay with it."

Some of the worry she'd been carrying melted away. "Thanks, Baby. I appreciate that." She drew him in for a hug and pulled his head down for a noisy kiss on the cheek. "I'm glad we sorted that out. I've gotta get back to work, and I'm sure you do too."

"Yeah. And we'll be by to pick up Otis this afternoon, to get him out of your hair. Thanks for keeping him. I hope he wasn't too much trouble."

She thought of the La Perla bra and thanked God that the puppy seemed to have a soft mouth. "He certainly kept me on my toes. He's a sweet thing, but I'll be glad to have my house back."

6

Over the next week and a half, winter really set in over Tennessee. Temperatures had been in the mid-twenties the past few nights, and it didn't look like today was going to get much above freezing. Grey hunched his shoulders against the cold as he hustled toward the door of the realty office. Magnolia had messaged that she had the perfect property for him, a listing in the next county over. A half-hour drive from Eden's Ridge was absolutely doable. He hoped the place fit the bill and the budget, because he was itching to get started on more than just the business plan for his new venture, and so were his connections in Washington. But he needed to be further along in the process before he met with them.

He tugged open the door and stepped inside.

A tall, harried black man turned wide eyes in his direction. "Are you Captain Greyson?"

"Yes?" He was so taken aback by the panic in the other man's face, it came out like a question.

The guy shoved a paper into his hands. "Good. You take this. Now she'll actually leave for the hospital."

Grey automatically took the paper. "I'm sorry. What's happening?"

But the guy was already sprinting down the hall. "Magnolia! He's here. Let's go."

A moment later Magnolia emerged from her office, one hand pressed to her back, the other on her protruding belly. "I swear, Calvin, I'm fine. There's plenty of time." Spotting Grey, she started to smile. "Captain Greyson. I apologize for the hoopla, but—" Her words cut off as her face twisted in pain.

"Breathe, baby." Calvin began to do that weird hissing breathing they always showed on TV during Lamaze classes.

Grey's head swam a little. "Dear God, is she in labor?"

"Yes, and she refused to leave for the hospital without talking to you first."

Now Calvin's panic made sense.

Magnolia blew out a slow breath. "Because we had an appointment."

Grey immediately stepped back. "We can certainly reschedule."

"Not necessary. Did Calvin give you the instructions for access?"

Glancing at the paper in his hand, he saw directions to some address and the codes for accessing some lockboxes. "Yes."

"I've already phoned the owner. He moved to Utah several months back and is fine with you touring the place on your own. He's a very motivated seller, so he's being extra cooperative. Not too many people want a property like his. It's a little outside the box and a little above your price range, but I'm pretty sure we can get him to accept a lower offer."

"Okay, message delivered. We're going." Calvin hustled his wife toward the door.

"I'm telling you, we've got plenty of time. Dion took ten hours to make his appearance."

Grey rushed to open it for them. They were still bickering about labor times as Calvin got his wife into the car. He rushed back to lock the door of the office. And then they were gone, leaving Grey alone at the curb feeling more than a little shell-shocked.

"So that happened." He muttered it to no one in particular and felt more than a little out of sorts.

As he was evidently on his own for the showing, he took a chance and called Rebecca, expecting to leave a message.

"Hey, you." Her warm voice filled the line, making him wish she was right here so he could reel her in for a kiss.

"Hey. I won't keep you, but what time do you get off today?"

"As it happens, my last client of the day rescheduled, and I always take off early on Fridays to do my grocery shopping, so I'm free."

"Want to come with me to look at some property?"

"Sure. I'm at the shop."

"I'll be by to get you in a few minutes."

When he pulled up in front, she hurried out, her bright crimson coat a pop of color against the otherwise gray day. She slid into the passenger seat and immediately leaned across the console to brush a kiss to his lips.

On a contented sigh, he smiled. "Hey, gorgeous."

Those familiar green eyes sparkled. "Hey, yourself. Where are we going?"

"Next county over. It's about two-hundred-fifty acres, and there's some kind of house. Guy that owns it moved out West, apparently."

"Okay, then. Is Magnolia meeting us there?"

"Magnolia is currently in labor."

Rebecca's mouth fell open. "What?"

As he headed out of town, he explained what had happened at the office.

"Oh, my God. That's such a Magnolia thing to do. But

Calvin was right to worry. Second babies almost always come faster."

"Did that happen for you?" It felt incredibly weird to ask her about something so personal as labor. But her kids were a huge part of her life. It seemed like something he maybe ought to know.

"Jonah took forever. Or what felt like forever, anyway. Nearly sixteen hours. Sam, on the other hand, was in a hurry. We barely made it to the hospital. They hadn't even finished my intake paperwork and had only *just* gotten me to a room."

Grey had no idea what to say to that.

Seemingly unconcerned, Rebecca leaned forward in her seat, eyeing the dark clouds. "With the cold we've been having, I can't help hoping there's snow in those clouds."

He didn't think they looked like snow clouds, but who was he to rain on her parade? The South loved their infrequent snow days. "You never know."

Conversation turned to other easier topics for the rest of the drive to the property. They only passed a handful of other cars on the way. The gate to the place was a little overgrown, with winter dark vines wrapped around the posts. But the lockbox worked as advertised, and he swung the gate open with ease. After driving through and shutting it behind them, he got back into the SUV.

"It's pretty remote out here," Rebecca observed.

"That may be a big part of why it's still on the market. Big property. Most people want to be closer to town. Seems like the road needs some work." It had been paved once, but was now a sad patchwork of potholes and cracks.

The trees closed in as they drove deeper onto the property, and though most were bare, they still seemed to cast a shadow. The entry road split in two directions. Based on the rudimentary map Magnolia had drawn, the left fork would take them toward the house and the right would circle through much of the acreage. He turned to the right, wanting to see whatever he could of the land.

As he'd requested, the terrain was varied. Thick sections of woods opened up to a mountain stream. It didn't have a ton of water flow just now, but he suspected in spring this section of road might actually be impassable. He'd need to build a bridge if he bought the place. They splashed across the stream and the road continued into an open meadow, and then began to rise as it entered another patch of woods.

"It's beautiful, if a little spooky."

"I think that's just the atmosphere of the weather." The clouds had darkened on their drive, and he was pretty sure it was gonna start raining soon. "I'll have to come back another time to more thoroughly check out the land itself. I think the weather's gonna turn. Let's find the house and have a look at it."

The drive leading up to the house had largely washed out. Grey switched into 4-wheel drive to make it up the steep grade. That was definitely a problem, and it didn't give him a lot of hope about the condition the building itself would be in. But as they topped the rise, they were greeted by an expanse of steel and glass. A modern sprawl of a house that would've been more at home in California than rural Tennessee.

Rebecca was the first to break the silence. "Wow. That's... something."

"Magnolia didn't mention the place was huge. I'm guessing three or four thousand square feet." As Grey parked in front of the house, rain began to spit. "Let's get on in and check it out. See whatever there is to see, and we'll check the radar. Maybe this storm will pass soon." It was something he should've checked himself before heading out here, but he'd been so distracted by Magnolia being in labor, he hadn't even thought to focus on practicalities.

They slipped out of the SUV and raced for the door. By the time he'd worked the lock box and retrieved the key, it was beginning to rain in earnest. Their footsteps echoed as they rushed into the house. Grey felt along the wall for the light switch. Nothing happened when he flipped it. "No power. Well, we can still see some from the light coming in the windows."

"Check this out." Rebecca stood before a massive stone fireplace. "What kind of person has a gorgeous fireplace like this and then pairs it with such a monstrosity of a faux fur rug?"

The asymmetrical rug was vaguely animal shaped, with long, dense "fur" in a truly horrific shade that might have been puce, but he didn't have enough light to be sure. "Somebody with cold feet?" At her smirk, he shrugged. "I don't know. Maybe a better question is, why is the rug the only thing left in the house?"

"Maybe when the house was packed up, it was accidentally-on-purpose forgotten."

"I mean, burning it seems like it would've been an easier way to get rid of it."

They wandered from room to room, confirming that there definitely was no other furniture in the place. The whole house had been designed to bring the outside in, a fact which was more than evident as they rapidly lost more light. Using the flashlights on their cell phones, they finished out the tour.

"It seems well-built." That was really the best he could tell without proper light.

"Do you like it?"

"I don't have to like it. It's a roof and all the basics. More than the basics. I've certainly survived in a lot worse, and I was prepared to live in a trailer for a while, if I had to. What do you think?" He hadn't come out here intending to look at this place as a potential future home with her, but walking through with her by his side made it impossible not to think about it.

"I mean, it's big. The views are probably gorgeous at least part of the year. It's super modern, but it could be warmed up with paint and softer furnishings. It just needs someone to turn it into a home. It feels like it never was one, you know?" As she met his gaze, a flash of lightning illuminated the room, followed by a clap of thunder so loud it shook the house.

"And I think that's our cue." Even as he said it, the telltale ping of sleet began to pound a staccato rhythm on the glass. "That is... not good." He tried pulling up the radar but didn't have enough signal. "Nothing. Do you have any bars?"

"Just one. Enough to get out a text, but probably not even enough for a phone call." She bit her lip as she looked out at the falling dark. "I know it's a little late to be asking this, but is it even safe for us to try to get down that mountain again in the dark and ice?"

"I'm inclined to say no. The temperatures have been below freezing for days. That ground is primed to freeze."

"What are we gonna do?"

"For now, we're gonna stay here. There's no electricity, but it's at least out of the wind and will provide more shelter than the Jeep. I don't think this storm is gonna let up any time soon."

"Is that going to be okay?"

"Well, we'll explain when we get back to civilization that we had to hang out. If the guy gets pissed about it, we can offer him some kind of compensation."

"So we're just going to hang out here in the dark?"

"It's better than sliding off the mountain on black ice. But I can do better than the dark. I'm gonna run out to the Jeep to grab some supplies, and I'm pretty sure I saw some wood stacked by the door when we came in. Meanwhile, see if you can get a text out to Jonah, so he knows not to worry. We may be stuck here for the night."

～

"I'M PRETTY SURE the flue is open. I'm gonna risk building a fire. Hold the light for me, will you?"

Rebecca took the flashlight Grey offered and trained the beam on the fireplace as he began to arrange the wood he'd brought inside.

The weather was getting worse. The mix of rain and sleet had shifted to sleet and snow. She could just barely make out the swirl of white beyond the glass. *Lovely.* Because, of course, in Tennessee they couldn't just get the pretty, fluffy snow. They had to get ice storms. Rebecca knew from lifelong experience that those could last for quite a while. Often days. While she wasn't opposed to being away from civilization for that long, she preferred such a getaway to be planned, with electricity and food more along the lines of s'mores and hot chocolate than the MREs Grey had in his emergency kit. Not that she was complaining about the bounty of supplies he'd brought in. They'd be fed, dry, and warm, which was a whole lot better than the alternative.

She turned her attention to the man himself as he gently coaxed a flame from the tinder he'd laid in. Because of course he had tinder in all those supplies, too.

"You're very prepared."

"It's a side effect of my former occupation. Be ready for anything. Technically, you could drop me in the middle of the wilderness with nothing but a knife, and I can survive just fine, but I prefer to be a bit more kitted out than that."

"This is all a far cry from when we all used to go up to Watauga Lake with nothing more than sleeping bags, hot dogs, and pilfered beer." The three of them and a handful of others had loaded up in a couple of pickups and driven out to camp under the stars. There'd been laughter and tipsy singing and ghost stories around the fire.

"Those were good summers." He fed a little more wood to the infant flame and glanced back with a grin. "Especially since you more or less lived in that blue bikini."

"You remember my bikini?"

"With vivid clarity. That summer you were sixteen was when I realized you were not simply one of my best friends. You were my best friend with breasts. I think it was inevitable that things would change after that. It was just a matter of time."

"Took you long enough."

He arranged the wood over the small flame, and they both watched it smoke.

"Would you have been open to something sooner?"

"Why do you think I paraded around in that bikini?"

Grey sat back on his heels. "The torture was on purpose?"

"Entirely."

They were a long way from summer and bikini weather now. Even in her coat, the chill of the house was soaking into her bones. She wrapped her arms around herself, careful to keep the light where he needed it.

"Cold?"

"Yeah."

Rising, he closed the distance between them, pulling her close and briskly rubbing her arms. In the fireplace beyond, she saw the wood begin to catch, heard it start to crackle.

"Looks like we have success. Good on you, Prometheus."

"I've built a fire or two in my day."

This wasn't what she'd expected when she'd come out here with him. She'd thought they'd have a quick adventure and come back to town, maybe go to dinner before returning to her house or his. But it wasn't all bad. They were alone out here, with no chance of interruption. No distractions. And he'd built her a fire. There was something weirdly primitive in the gesture. Caretaking at the most basic level. As the flame began to catch, she thought it would be a shame to let that go to waste.

Apparently mistaking her silence for concern, Grey gave her a squeeze. "Once it's daylight, I'll be able to see what we're working with for getting down the mountain. We'll be okay."

She flattened her palm against his chest. "No, I know we'll be fine. I'm here with you. In this big, empty house, where no one's going to find us or interrupt us."

The hands that had been rubbing warmth back into her arms slowed. "Yeah, that's true."

Her lips twitched. "The fire will help eventually, but it's a big space. I think we'll probably have to share body heat."

"That is an option." His eyes glinted in the faint light from the growing fire.

"I mean, it's practically mandated in the handbook."

"Which handbook would that be?"

"Literally any romance novel involving the protagonists being snowed in." Of which she'd read dozens. It was one of her favorite tropes.

He tightened his hold, sliding his arms around to her back. "What else is in this handbook?"

"Well, there's the necessity of stripping off wet clothes. So you don't get hypothermia." Tossing the flashlight toward the rug, she unbuttoned his coat, sliding her hands inside and over his shoulders to shove it off.

"Definitely can't have that." His own fingers made quick work of her buttons and the knot on the belt of her coat. Then it joined his on the bamboo floor.

Pressing closer, she skimmed her hands up his chest, into the hair that was damp from the rain.

They'd both been wet from the lake that first time. He'd followed her when she dove in, and she'd wrapped around him, daring to take the kiss she'd yearned for. She could see the memory of that day in his eyes as he stared down at her. There'd been hesitance and wonder in the boy as they'd fumbled their way into being lovers under a bower of branches on the grassy bank. Now she saw only hunger and certainty in the man as he lowered his mouth to hers.

A contented sigh rose from her toes at the contact, and she

melted into him as he took her in a long, drugging kiss. She'd never get tired of this. Didn't think she could ever make up for all those missed years without it. But she absolutely wanted to try.

When he pulled back, she whimpered in protest.

"Wait just a minute."

She swayed as he stepped away. With quick, practiced moves, he'd opened the sleeping bag, spreading it out over the rug. When he offered his hand, she took it without hesitation, following him over to the nest he'd made. The heart beating slow and thick in her chest stumbled a little as he knelt at her feet, carefully removing her ankle boots. He slipped off his own shoes, and they stepped onto the sleeping bag.

As a rule, she was pretty comfortable in her own skin. She appreciated her body for everything it did for her, but she was still grateful this first time would happen by firelight. Flattering and romantic.

His callused palms slid beneath her sweater, skimming the skin at her waist as he drew her close again. She shivered at the touch, needing so much more. He pressed a kiss to her brow. Soft. Fleeting. Her eyes drifted shut as he continued to her temple, her cheek, and on down to her throat. Tipping her head back for him, she held on and basked in sensation.

"I want to kiss you everywhere."

At the confession, she shuddered. "Yes, please." She wanted that. Wanted him. But the trembling didn't stop.

"You okay?" he murmured, nuzzling her ear.

"Yes."

"If any of this gets to be too much, tell me to stop."

"Don't stop." No matter what else happened between them, she needed this.

They lost themselves in the deliberate dance of exploration, stripping away far more than mere clothing. The fire cast a warm glow over each inch of newly exposed skin. His chest was a thing of beauty. Hardened and honed over years. She ran her hands over it before leaning forward to close her lips over one round nipple.

Grey made some inarticulate noise. "I'm gonna need you to table that for a bit."

"Why?"

"Because I've waited more than thirty years for this, and I'm not going to rush it."

So chastened, she didn't fight as he laid her back on the sleeping bag, following her down. He took his mouth on a lazy journey down her bare torso, his hands and mouth exploring. Rebecca's nerve endings sang with each new sensation. She was no stranger to pleasure. Over the years, she'd gotten very comfortable and acquainted with taking care of herself in that department. But it was a very, very different thing to have a partner. Particularly one she wanted as much as he wanted her.

As his tongue circled one nipple, her hips bowed up. She felt his smile against her skin as he did it again, pulling that tight peak into his mouth. When the hand at her waist didn't move, she took the initiative herself, boldly dragging his hand between her thighs and cupping it there. At the warmth and pressure, she moaned, all but ready to vibrate out of her skin.

"What do you need?"

She hesitated only a moment. What good was all that intimate knowledge of what aroused her if she didn't share it?

"Stroke me."

One finger drew through her folds, spreading the moisture there.

Grey gave a low curse, pressing his hips against hers so she could feel his erection behind his fly. "You're so wet."

"Give me your finger."

Obediently, he slipped one inside.

She gasped at the sensation. Oh, that was glorious. But it could be even better. With one hand, she reached to position him, guiding his thumb to circle her clit. Her head fell back as he began to pump his fingers, finding a rhythm with her hips, even as his mouth continued to do wonderful, wicked things to her breasts.

"Another," she moaned.

He added a second finger, and oh, the fullness was too much and not enough. Her body quaked and bucked, seeking that last little push over the edge. Shifting, he bore down, giving her some of his weight as she rode his hand.

The orgasm detonated on a scream, spiraling out from her center and shattering every piece of her with what felt like endless shockwaves.

Sometime later, she managed to drag in more than a gasping breath and opened her eyes to find him staring down at her, his head propped on his hand.

"I'd be happy watching you do that for the rest of my life."

The heart that had begun to slow kicked up speed again. He looked absolutely, deadly serious. But she wasn't prepared for everything that meant. Not with her defenses laid to waste.

She worked up a coquettish smile, hoping to distract him. "Well, I really hope you plan to do more than watch."

"Oh, I absolutely do."

Rolling toward him, she reached for his zipper. "Then let me help you with that."

It was his turn to gasp and moan as she freed him from his jeans, taking him in her hand. With an appreciative caress, she circled her thumb around his crown, soaking up the sensation of velvet skin over all that hardness. She'd almost forgotten what the real thing was like.

"Rebel, if you don't want this over before it starts, you'll stop that right now."

He solved the matter by flipping her onto her back. She welcomed the weight and warmth of him, tipping her mouth up to his for another long, greedy kiss. Hooking one leg around his, she pressed her hips into his, seeking that hardness.

"Wait just... a..." Grey groped for where his pants had landed, fishing out a condom.

He ripped it open, rolled it on, then he was back in the cradle of her hips, his cock nudging her entrance. Pausing there, he framed her face in his hands, just staring down at her. "This."

"What?"

"This is everything I've been missing. You're everything I've been missing."

On that pronouncement, he pressed inside. She cried out, as much in response to the sudden fullness of her body as her heart.

He froze. "Did I hurt you?"

"No." Because the tears gathering in her eyes called her a liar, she framed his face in return. "No. Don't stop."

As he began to move, she kissed him again, feeling the tremor start so much deeper than her core. With every stroke, she simultaneously coiled tighter and opened wider. Here was completion. The rightness she'd never felt with anyone but him. They barreled toward the edge of bliss together, and she wrapped tight around him. He'd been her first. And as they tipped into mutual insanity, she hoped to God he'd be her last.

7

There was nothing like sleeping on a cold, hard floor to make Grey feel every single one of his fifty-three years. And nothing like being curled up with a warm, naked Rebel to make every ache well worth it. She slept the sleep of the thoroughly sated, head tucked against his shoulder, arm draped over his torso, legs tangled with his. Not that she could've gone anywhere, wedged as they were into the sleeping bag that was really meant for one. He'd zipped them in some-time after they'd exhausted themselves and he'd added the last of the logs to the fire.

That fire was out now, and sunlight crept across the floor to their pallet, illuminating the gold undertones in Rebecca's rich, dark hair. The storm was over. He couldn't tell from here what kind of aftermath they'd be dealing with or whether they could get back to town. All of it could wait. He wanted to soak in every shred of pleasure in waking up with her. They'd never been able to do this when they were teenagers. If they had, he didn't know if he'd have been able to leave her. Then again, maybe it was all the years apart that made him appreciate the simple joy of having her wrapped around him. It sure as hell wasn't something he'd take for granted.

So he ignored the fact that his ass was numb and his shoulder would almost certainly scream the moment he moved it, in favor of breathing in the sleep-warmed scent of her and wondering how long he'd have to wait to make this permanent.

Full-steam ahead, Captain.

Before his brain could go too far into that fantasy, she stretched against him, then went very still as her eyes blinked open. The hand at his waist flexed. "You're here."

"I am."

Her fingers traced down over the curve of his bare hip. "Not a dream."

"Nope."

A pretty flushed worked its way up her cheeks as she looked anywhere but at him.

"Why are you getting shy now? You didn't have any problem being direct last night."

The blush deepened, and she pressed her face into his shoulder. "Last night I was..."

Wanting to reassure, he curled a hand around her nape and rubbed. "Incredibly hot. I liked you ordering me around." Even thinking of it had his cock standing at attention, reporting for duty.

"Well, I know what I like."

"Which is fucking glorious, and I want to learn everything that falls into that category, in great detail, as soon as humanly possible."

That drew a laugh out of her. "Maybe let's consider doing that in a bed. At home."

"See also the part about as soon as humanly possible."

"Then we'd better get dressed and see what the state of the road is."

Accepting they couldn't stay cocooned in the sleeping bag

forever, he braced himself to face the cold. Moving fast, he unzipped one side and rolled away from her, tucking the edge back down to retain whatever heat he could. Biting back a curse as his shoulder protested the movement, he dove for his pants. He'd yanked them on and was reaching for his sweater when he heard her gasp.

"Grey!"

"What? What's wrong?"

She scrambled up, circling around him to lay her hands on his back, over the scars. "What...?"

"It's nothing. I'm fine." And he was. Mostly.

Her fingers traced the ridges of tissue. "This isn't nothing."

Turning to face her, he drew her in, brushing a kiss to her brow. "Just battle scars. Get dressed. It's too cold for your birthday suit if I'm not in mine."

Her hands fell away as he dragged on his sweater. Making quick work of his socks and boots, he snagged his coat and headed outside.

It was the view, rather than the cold, that stole his breath. Morning sun struck the ice-covered trees, making them sparkle like jewels. The winter wonderland was beautiful. And it was already melting. A patter of falling drops sounded around him, a bass beat to the mix of snow and ice that crunched beneath his boots as he strode toward the drive. More snow and ice fell off the Jeep as he popped the back hatch and reached in for his trekking poles.

Moving carefully, he made his way down the slope, examining the rutted driveway. The ice would definitely be a problem for a while longer, but it looked like temperatures would continue to rise, melting the accumulation. If they were careful, they could probably manage by late morning. Climbing the hill again, Grey circled around the house and found another road, this one in better condition, leading into another copse of woods. The garage was on this side, and there was no drive leading around from the front. Apparently, this was the actual driveway.

"Son of a bitch."

Rebecca was dressed by the time he came back inside, her hair gathered up into a knot. Her eyes were worried, her posture a little uncertain. Hating that, he closed the distance between them and wrapped her in his arms.

"Well, there's good news and bad news."

"Good news first."

"The good news is that stuff is already melting, so there's no question we'll be able to get out of here today."

"A good thing. I think the boys were about to mount a rescue mission. I've been given strict instructions to let them know when I make it back."

"Oh, were you able to get a text out last night?"

"I'm not sure when it finally sent. There was a stack waiting for me when I got up. I told them we were fine, and that you were working on digging out the Jeep."

Grey took a moment to be grateful they hadn't been interrupted by a three-man rescue team. He didn't really want to think about how her trio of sons would react to finding them naked together.

"What's the bad news?"

"We maybe didn't have to spend the night out here last night at all. The real driveway is off the back of the house. And unlike what we came in on, it looks like it's been paved this century."

"So... we camped out on a hard floor for no reason?"

He laced his hands at the small of her back and grinned. "Well, I wouldn't say no reason. Whether I buy the place or not, I might have to make an offer on the rug."

With a look of abject horror, she thumped him on the shoulder. "Oh my God, don't you dare."

"What? We could have it dyed a more pleasing color."

"Mitchell."

He winced at the exasperated tone. "Trotting out the first name. Fine. We'll leave the rug. But I'm still happy about last night."

On a sigh, she snuggled against him. "Me, too."

"Let's eat something and take a better tour of the house, now that it's light. Then we'll see about getting back to town."

"To a shower," she sighed. "There is only so much I can do with wet wipes from my purse."

"Fair enough. I shall endeavor to get you back for a shower as soon as possible." And if he was lucky, she'd let him join her.

An hour later, they were rolling slowly down the driveway, headed back toward town. Grey wasn't sure if it was the daylight or the sex, but the whole property looked better today. The house had potential, and certainly the land itself would do for what he had in mind. As soon as Magnolia was able, he'd put in an offer and see whether the owner would come to terms. If he needed to bump things up a bit, he had a willing investor on the hook.

They rolled into Eden's Ridge during prime Saturday breakfast hour. Despite the chill in the air, a line stretched outside the diner as they drove by.

"Where did you leave your car?"

"It's at home, actually. I walked to work yesterday."

Three minutes later, he pulled into her driveway and shut off the engine.

"Well, that was an adventure." Her smile was a little tired around the edges.

"The first of many, I hope." Grey slid out of the driver's seat and hurried around to open her door.

The hand she placed in his felt like a promise. Or maybe that was just wishful thinking on his part. He walked her to the door, waiting as she unlocked it.

"So, I have a proposal."

"What's that?"

"You're tired. I'm tired. I suggest we go inside and make use of your shower—preferably together, as that's the environmentally responsible thing to do—and then fall into your bed for a nap and... other things for the rest of the day."

Her eyes kindled. She leaned in, her lips curving as one hand fisted on the lapel of his jacket. "I think—"

He didn't get to find out what she thought because a truck pulled into the driveway beside his Jeep.

By the time Jonah stepped out, Grey thought he had the lust locked down. Mostly.

"You okay?" The question was divided between them, but Jonah's eyes were entirely for his mother.

"Yeah, I'm fine. We had a roof over our head. There was a fireplace, so we were warm. And we had MREs. I'll never think they're *good*, but they served their purpose. We're just tired. I'm not used to sleeping on the hard floor."

Grey worked to keep his expression neutral. *Do* not *think about all the not sleeping we did last night. Do* not.

"Fair enough. You should have time for a solid nap before meeting Rachel to work on the wedding favors this evening. Or do you need to reschedule?"

"That's today? What am I saying? Of course, it's today. The wedding's in a week. I may be a little late, but I'll be there."

Recognizing that his own plans for the day were firmly derailed, Grey shifted gears. "I'm gonna get out of your way so you can get some rest. I've got a few things to take care of." He leaned in to brush a kiss over her lips, as much because he wanted to as to make a point in front of her son. The spark of heat in her eyes as he pulled back was gratifying. "Call you later, okay?"

"Okay."

He headed for his Jeep, nodding at her son. "Jonah."

"Grey."

The wary tone almost made him laugh. Almost.

Spinning on his heel, he walked backward. "Oh, hey, where can I buy a baby gift in this town? I figure Magnolia's new one's here by now."

"Try Moonbeams and Sweet Dreams downtown," Rebecca suggested. "If Misty doesn't have anything, she'll know where Magnolia's registered."

"Thanks." On a wave, he slid into the driver's seat.

His brain was already working through all the details he needed to put into place so he could make this move home official and permanent. That was the first stage in making a life with her that was permanent.

"OKAY, one of you fell down on your job of stopping me from getting lost in the black hole that is Pinterest," Rachel announced. "*Why* did I decide that homemade soaps and custom handmade party boxes were a good idea?"

"Because you've got a limited guest list, and you wanted to give it a personal touch," Cayla informed her. "And as it is actually a lovely idea, it was my job as your wedding planner to encourage that."

"Besides, many hands make light work." Rebecca narrowed her eyes as she carefully cut around the edges of the template that would ultimately be one of the party boxes.

"I really appreciate you coming to help. After last night, you totally didn't have to."

"I'm happy to help."

Mia carefully pre-folded one of the boxes. "How *was* last night? I swear, I thought Brax was going to pace a hole in the floor."

"Holt wasn't any better. I overheard him on the phone with Jonah debating about whether anybody in the area had a snowmobile. As if we ever get enough snow in Tennessee to justify one of those."

"Jonah was thinking more horseback. If you'd been any closer, I'm pretty sure he'd have come after you."

Rebecca rolled her eyes. "Oh, for heaven's sake. You'd think I was a teenage ingenue, the way they're all acting. I'm a grown-ass woman. It's not like I was trapped with the big bad wolf."

Cayla tied off one of the fully assembled boxes with the blue and silver ribbon that matched the wedding colors. "Well, to be fair, given how Grey looks at you, I don't think that's too far from the truth."

Heat burned in Rebecca's cheeks, and she turned all her focus to her cutting. "*That* is none of their business."

Mia threw back her head and laughed. "Good for you!" She lifted her glass of sparkling cider. "Here's to breaking long dry spells."

Rebecca shot an apprehensive glance around the table as all three girls lifted their glasses. "Please don't mention that to the boys. They might do something stupid like corner him."

"We would never," Cayla assured her.

"We are duty-bound to redirect our men so they don't interfere," Rachel added.

Remembering how she'd jumped in to help distribute the rest of the Christmas crackers at dinner, Rebecca offered a when-in-Vegas shrug and lifted her own glass in a toast.

Cayla drank and set down her glass. "Hopefully, they'll have all worked off some frustration with that town-wide cleanup of trees downed by the ice storm and will be chilled out again by the time they get home."

"Here's hoping." Mia resumed pre-folding the boxes. "As someone who also got married right out of high school, I'm supercurious—was this a surprise to you, or was there some kind of love triangle situation going on back then between you and Lonnie and Grey?"

She definitely didn't want to get into that. "Grey and I were very close when we were younger, but we wanted different things out of life. Neither of us knew how to compromise, so at eighteen, that was the end of that. Now we're both older and theoretically wiser, so we're exploring the road not taken. Whatever that looks like."

Cayla heaved a dramatic sigh. "I love a good second chance romance. Have you asked him to the wedding yet?"

"I hadn't actually thought about it. I figured I'd be mostly tied up and hadn't thought about a date." Though, now that she mentioned it, Rebecca really wanted to see Grey in a suit.

As the conversation turned to a cheerful discussion of all the reasons she ought to ask him, Rebecca noted her future daughter-in-law had gone awfully quiet. She filed that away to address when they'd wrapped for the night.

"Okay, this is the last one!" Cayla finished tying the bow and threw up her hands, as if she were a calf roper in a rodeo. "We are *done*, and I need to get home for the bedtime routine. If I'm not there to cut it off, Maddie will have Holt singing about eleven million bedtime songs."

Mia shoved back from the table. "I'm out, too. Dakota will go down fine, but Duncan usually only wants me at bedtime."

"I'll stick around to help clean up. Give all those sweet babies second-hand grandma hugs."

"We absolutely will," Mia promised.

After another round of hugs and thank yous, the two women headed out, leaving Rebecca alone with Rachel.

She began gathering up paper scraps for the garbage. "Are you okay? You seem like something's on your mind."

Rachel knit her fingers together. "Yeah. Yeah, there is."

Sensing she needed some support, Rebecca eased back down in a chair. "Do you want to talk about it?" This whole wedding had to be bringing up a lot of memories and feelings about her first husband, who'd died a few years before as a result of a traumatic brain injury sustained on his job as a fire-fighter.

A furrow dug in between her brows, betraying her sense of disquiet. "I really do. I've been thinking about this a lot for the past few weeks."

Oh, boy. Keeping her voice gentle, Rebecca laid a hand over hers. "Are you having second thoughts about the wedding?"

"No! No, it's nothing like that. But it does have to do with Jonah." The sheer concern in her expression had an alarm bell beginning to clang somewhere deep in Rebecca's brain.

"Does he have more of a problem with me dating Grey than he's said?"

Rachel pressed her lips into a thin line, obviously considering her words. "That's complicated."

"Complicated how?"

"So, you know how, when you're with somebody for a really long time, you notice all these little quirks about them? Body language. Birthmarks. Just the sort of little things most people don't consciously register."

"Sure." When Rachel said nothing, Rebecca pushed. "What is it, honey?"

"It's just... I'm trying to find the right way to say this."

"Just spit it out." Whatever it was would be easier to deal with once it was out there.

Distress highlighted Rachel's blue eyes, and she went back to linking her fingers together. "Please know that this is not about offending you or accusing you, but I just have to know."

Rebecca's heart began to pound. She was out of time.

"I thought, at first, that Grey reminded me of Jonah just because he was also a SEAL and they had the same kind of training. They move the same way. But I kept looking at Grey during Christmas dinner. Everyone says Jonah looks just like you—and he does, to a point. But I think that's what everyone defaults to because you're who was here for comparison." Rachel stared at her, eyes begging her to understand.

Damn it. Damn it! She should have already talked to Grey. She'd put it off, telling herself they deserved the uncomplicated time to find their way back together. And they had. But this was not how she'd wanted this to go. None of the scenarios she'd considered involved someone figuring it out before she'd had the chance to voice the truth herself.

Swallowing hard, she managed to keep her voice level. "Have you talked to Jonah about any of this?"

Jonah hadn't shown up demanding explanations, so she was pretty sure the answer was no.

Rachel shook her head. "No. The truth is better coming from you. But I need to know—is Jonah Grey's son?"

8

There was nothing like hard physical labor to clear the head. After picking up a baby gift for Magnolia and a productive call to Ned Maguire, his contact in Washington, Grey found himself pitching in to clear the debris left by the ice storm. It wasn't the afternoon of napping and debauchery he'd have preferred, but it was a solid use of his time. He was moving home. He needed to start putting himself out there and reintegrating back into the community.

He'd been unsurprised to find Jonah and his friends as part of the impromptu crew. While all three men gave him wary looks, none of them started anything. Grey figured that was progress. The four of them naturally gravitated into a team, running chainsaws, hauling tree limbs, clearing roads. As day bled into night, most of the workforce began to peel off to head home.

Holt was the first of their group to call it. "I gotta go pick up Maddie and rescue my mother-in-law, since Cayla's with the rest of the women tonight."

"I'm sure not gonna leave our two with Donna on their own." Brax tugged off his gloves. "I'll come with you."

Other than lifting a hand to wave, Jonah didn't stop what he was doing.

Pausing to guzzle down some more water, Grey eyed the long stretch of downed fence along the north side of Percy Gibbons's farm. The row of trees that had taken it out had been removed. Chunks of tree trunk still needed to be hauled off and wire restrung to ensure none of Percy's cows wandered off. The fencing materials were already waiting for the job. "You know whether Percy's got his cattle corralled for the night?"

Jonah hefted another chunk of the tree into the back of his truck. "He does for now, but he'll want to let them out after milking tomorrow."

"You ready to stop for the night, or you want to keep going? Shouldn't take more than an hour or two to restring those fences."

"Given the alternative is making some fussy, handmade gift box thing back at my house, I'll take the fence."

Grey huffed a laugh. "I'll move my Jeep around so we can see."

He parked so that the headlights illuminated the stretch of fencing, and the two of them got to work. They fell into a rhythm, attaching wire, stretching it to the next post, fastening it, then doing it all over again on down the line. Grey wasn't uneasy with the silence, but as it was just the two of them, he thought he ought to make an effort at conversation. Maybe it would help get them over the hump of this new weirdness between them.

"You getting excited about the wedding?"

"I'm ready to be married and get on with the business of life. In a month or two, they'll be starting the dirt work on the new house."

"Y'all are building?"

"Yeah, out on the site of my great grandmother's old house.

It burned down last year, so we cleared the land. Just been waiting until Mia and her crew can get to it."

"Pretty spot out there. I liked your great grandmother."

"You knew her?"

"Oh, yeah. She made the absolute best chocolate chip cookies. When we were young, Lonnie and I did a hell of a lot of yard work for her in exchange for those cookies."

"I'll have to see if Mom has the recipe. We can try them out at the bakery."

"They're sure to be a best seller." Grey hammered in the next fencing staple. "Are you happy at the bakery? With this whole new life you've built here?"

Jonah glanced at him over the post. "Are you asking as a former CO or as somebody who's in the same boat starting over?"

"Both."

He unspooled the wire, walking it to the next post. "It's not the life I expected." The long pause was filled with the sounds of metal bending and wire sliding over wood. "But yeah. I get to work with two of my best friends every day. I met a woman I'm crazy about, who's crazy enough to want to spend the rest of her life with me. I'm not risking life and limb on the daily. I feel pretty fucking lucky all around to get a shot at all that." Getting a grip on the wire, he stretched it around the post, pulling it taut. "Do you regret missing all of that?"

Grey placed the next staple and pounded it in to give himself a few moments to think. "I believed in the work we did. Is there a part of me that wishes I'd had a wife and family to come home to in between missions? Yeah. But I think that would've made doing my duty harder."

"And now?"

In the relative darkness, Grey couldn't read the expression in Jonah's eyes, but he felt the weight of the younger man's gaze.

"Now, I feel really fucking fortunate that your mom is giving me a shot."

The words hung in the air between them, eclipsing everything else for just a moment.

"You seem to make her happy." Jonah's grudging admission was accompanied by a wry smile.

Grey returned it. "I'm trying my level best."

"That's more than Lonnie managed. I know he had reasons, but—" Jonah shook his head. "She deserves to be happy." He loosed a long breath and met Grey's eyes. "So do you."

On that pronouncement, Jonah lapsed back into silence and began to string the final strand of barbed wire. Grey felt as if they'd turned some kind of corner. He'd take whatever progress he could get. Once they'd finished, he gathered up the remaining fencing supplies and tools while Jonah called to tell the very grateful Percy that his pasture was secure again.

As he ended the call, Grey's stomach gave an audible rumble.

Jonah lifted one brow. "How long's it been since you ate?"

"Lunch, I guess." He'd been too consumed with the work to think much about food.

"Why don't you come on back to the house? I can't make any promises about what's in our fridge, but there is absolute certainty Rachel made something for dinner. And there's definitely beer. I think we've earned one."

"I definitely won't turn it down. Whatever she made is better than the sandwich or can of soup I'd be opening back at my place."

"Come on, then."

Grey followed him back into town proper and out the other side, a few miles up into the mountains where Jonah and Rachel were renting a house. Seeing Rebel's car still in the drive had his mood lifting. His afternoon plans might've gotten derailed, but maybe they could be replaced with overnight plans instead.

Trailing Jonah to the front door, they both stopped to slip off their filthy work boots before going inside. Through a cased doorway, he could just make out some kind of hutch thing with neat stacks of boxes tied with pretty ribbon. Looked like the women had finished their project for the wedding. The low sound of voices came from that direction. The tone was soft, serious. Maybe Rachel and Rebecca were having a pre-wedding heart to heart. Grey hoped he and Jonah wouldn't be interrupting.

As they got closer, Rachel's voice came clearer. "I need to know—is Jonah Grey's son?"

Ahead of him, Jonah stopped dead in his tracks. So did Grey.

Someone—Rebecca?—inhaled a shuddering breath.

"Yes." The whispered response went off like a bomb.

Grey felt his world tilt.

His *son.*

He'd suspected. He'd hoped, even though that fact would rewrite everything he'd thought he'd known about his relationship with Rebecca. Joy and relief shot through him at the confirmation. He had a *son.* And not some stranger. A man he knew well and respected. A man he was proud of. A man he'd helped nurture and foster because somewhere deep down, maybe he'd already known.

That man was frozen half a dozen paces from the kitchen doorway, his face etched with the same kind of confusion Grey had seen on the battlefield in the wake of a concussive blast. He started to step forward, reaching out to touch him, but Jonah surged into the kitchen.

"What the *fuck?*"

Grey didn't actually think Jonah would get violent, but instinct had him rushing in, positioning himself to intercept him. Rebecca made some small, choked sound, all the color leeching from her cheeks. She looked from her son—*their son* —to him and simply closed her eyes, her face twisted in pain. Of course, this wasn't how she'd have wanted this to come out. Grey didn't know if she'd ever have admitted it on her own if she hadn't been asked outright. But that was a question for later. In the moment, there wasn't room for anything but the tsunami of Jonah's reaction.

The boy's hands were fisted. "How the hell could you lie about something like this?"

She flinched as if he'd struck her, and it took everything Grey had to stand still and let things unfold. Jonah had every right to his rage.

"Did Dad know?"

Grey noted the shift from Lonnie to Dad.

"Yeah."

What had Lonnie thought about raising another man's child? *His* child.

"Is that why he left? Why he wanted nothing to do with us? Because he found out?"

Her eyes peeled wide. "What? No! Your dad leaving had nothing to do with this. He knew from the beginning, and he never loved you any less."

A muscle ticked in Jonah's jaw as he turned a frustrated gaze on Grey. "You don't look surprised. Did you know?"

"I suspected."

What little color had come back into Rebecca's cheeks drained out again. He read so much pain and apology in her eyes.

"Before or after you came back here?" Jonah demanded.

Grey swung his attention back to his son. "Before. I'd always felt a kinship with you. I chalked it up to the fact that you were Rebecca's. It was, in a small way, a means of maintaining a connection I missed. But I didn't notice the similarities until I was going through all my parents' stuff. In the face, you look so much like your mother, but there are other physical character-istics, like that cowlick swirl on the back of your head, that are just like my dad. So I started to wonder."

"Is that why you came back?" Rebecca whispered.

He looked at her, seeing shades of the girl she'd been, the one he'd loved so much. "Partly. I wanted to know. But I came back for you. For a shot at what we both walked away from all those years ago."

Tears streamed down her cheeks, and her voice was ragged as she spoke again. "I tried to tell you. New Year's Eve, when we were clearing the air about our fight. But you didn't want to talk about the past anymore, and I didn't want to destroy what we were starting."

He thought back to that night. To her earnest, worried expression. *Grey, I need to tell you—*

He'd cut her off, making assumptions. What would he have done if she'd pressed on and revealed the truth then? Would it have changed anything? He supposed that depended on the details.

"Tell us now."

"Fuck that!" Jonah exploded.

Rachel stepped into his path, into the line of emotional fire. "Jonah, simmer down."

"How the hell can anyone expect me to calm down? My whole fucking life has been a lie."

She framed his face. "Let her explain."

"Explain? How can there be a reasonable explanation for this?"

Every harsh syllable had Rebecca curling in on herself. She'd been wrong to keep the secret, but she didn't deserve this ambush. Hearing her side of the story had to be the first step toward sorting this shit, and that meant Jonah had to reel in his reaction.

"Ferguson! Find some fucking decorum!" His thundered order reverberated through the kitchen.

Jonah snapped to attention, years of training overcoming his emotional outburst, even as he aimed a baleful glare at Grey. "You aren't my CO anymore."

"I don't give a good damn. Sit. Down."

SICK AND SHAKING, Rebecca watched the standoff. For a long moment, it looked as if Jonah was going to mouth off, but Grey simply waited, unblinking, every inch the commander he'd been trained to be. Resentment rolled off her boy in waves, but at last, Jonah sucked in a slow breath and reached for a chair. His arms were crossed, his jaw dialed to belligerent, but he sat. Rachel dropped into the chair next to him, close but not touching. Grey took the last seat, close enough Rebecca could've reached out to touch him.

But she didn't dare. She didn't know if she'd have the right after this.

Struggling to find some kind of control, she wiped at the tears. "Grey and I were together the summer after high school."

"Were you with Dad, too?

This was what her son thought of her? That she'd sleep with both of them at once? Fighting down the insult of that, she simply answered with the truth.

"We've already told you that Lonnie, Grey, and I were the three musketeers all through childhood. By the time we hit high school, that dynamic started to change. Everybody was growing up, and life wasn't quite as simple as it had been. I don't know quite when I realized that Grey and I had chemistry. It didn't matter. When I was around him, there was always Lonnie as the buffer. Lonnie to remind me of the consequences of upsetting the status quo. Then his cousin got him a job working construction down in Nashville for the summer. It was good money, so he left for a few months to do that, and Grey and I were still here, spending all our time together like we always had. But without that buffer, there was nothing to stop all that tension that had been simmering between us from changing things."

Was this how Grey remembered it? Rebecca couldn't bring herself to look at him to check.

Jonah made a disgusted noise. "Spare me the gory details."

"You're the one who demanded to know if I was with Lonnie at the same time, like I was some kind of revolving door, so you can damned well sit still and listen," she snapped. "It wasn't cheap or tawdry. We were best friends. Then we became more."

She'd been determined to take the chance. To find out if that heat would flare up, then out, or if it was the embers of something so much bigger. She hadn't been prepared for the explosion of that kiss. Hadn't expected the joy and excitement of first lust and love to consume them so quick and fast. But she hadn't regretted it. Not for a moment.

"We didn't exactly define things, but we were inseparable after that. Everything just felt like it was falling into place. There was the lingering question of how we were going to tell Lonnie when he got back, but we never really talked about it. We were more pulled into long, deep talks about life. About what was really important."

"That was what sent me to the recruiter's office."

At Grey's quiet confession, she dared to look and saw the raw pain in his eyes.

"What?"

"I wanted to be more than I had been. For you. I wanted to be worthy."

She hadn't thought she could bleed any more from this. But she'd been wrong. "Grey." For a moment, she had to close her eyes to get her emotions under control. "I wish you'd told me before. God, I wish we'd actually communicated about so many things."

"He didn't tell you until after he'd enlisted?" Rachel's quiet interjection reminded her of why she was telling this story.

"No, he didn't tell me about the Navy ROTC scholarship until just before he left in August. I didn't take it well. I saw my whole life here. I couldn't imagine a life of moving from one naval base to another, uprooting our family all the time, having the father of my children gone for months at a time. I didn't want to imagine it."

"You already knew about me?" Jonah demanded.

"No. Not then. But family was what I always wanted. It was something we'd talked about in the future we imagined. The one I thought we both wanted. But he was moving to the other side of the state, and the terms of the scholarship meant he'd be gone every summer. We wouldn't get to see each other beyond the occasional holiday, and I wanted more than that. I just knew that if he got a taste of life somewhere else, he'd never want to come back to me. So we fought, split up, and he left."

So many bitter words and so much heartache. And that had been only the beginning.

"His parents moved by Labor Day, eliminating any reason for him to come home, and I thought that was it. He had no more ties here. It was nearly October by the time I realized I was pregnant. I was so scared, and I felt so alone, and I didn't know what to do." Though it felt like slicing open a vein, she knew she owed Grey the respect of looking him in the eye.

"I knew if I told you, you'd come back. You'd do right by me. You'd give up your dream and be trapped. You didn't want the small town family life that I did. And even if we could've somehow figured out a way to make that work, you'd have lost your ROTC scholarship and your shot at college. All I could see if I told you was that I'd be putting you in a cage and giving you a million and one reasons to resent me. And potentially the child we'd made. I didn't want that for any of us."

If he understood her reasons, accepted them, he didn't show it. "How did Lonnie come into it?"

"He found me up at the lake. I went there a lot after you left. He knew I was upset about something and poked at me until I spilled everything. When I finished, he asked me to marry him. He argued that he wanted what I wanted. That he'd loved me for a long time. He knew I didn't feel the same—not beyond friendship—but he was willing to gamble that we'd grow into it in time. And either way, he wanted to do right by the brother of his heart, so you could go chase your dream. So I said yes."

"That must've torn you in two," Rachel murmured.

"Every day. But we got married. I never told Grey, and as far as I knew, he never came back, so I thought I made the right choice for all of us. There was never a reason to bring it up."

"Not a reason?" Jonah snarled. "You let me believe for *years* that he was my father. That I came from that weak, spineless excuse for a man."

With every word, Rebecca's heart cracked open further.

"Honey, what good would it have done you, after Lonnie and I split, for me to suddenly bring up the fact that you had another biological father out there who didn't even know you existed? We had no idea how he would react to you. I didn't know where he was or what he was doing. I didn't know if he was still in the Navy, and honestly, I was afraid to look because I didn't want to know what kind of life he'd built without me."

Because they were shaking, she knit her fingers together, determined to push through to the end. "But after all this time, he did come back. And I knew I had to tell you both. But I didn't know how. I kept hoping I'd come up with the right words, the right way to say it."

"There's no right way, no easy way, to drop this on us, Mom.

But sitting on it has to be one of the worst." Jonah's eyes were hard and furious. She'd seen this look on his face before, but never directed at her.

"I know you're angry, and you have every right to be. I know keeping this secret was wrong, but you need to understand that I was eighteen years old and scared to death. I made a decision, and I've lived with the consequences of that decision every day for more than thirty years. So please take that into account before you condemn me."

Jonah exploded out of his chair. "I need some air."

He prowled out the way he'd come. When the front door slammed, Rebecca flinched as if it were a gunshot. Heart hammering, she looked to Grey, who'd said next to nothing. She couldn't read his expression, and that was almost worse than Jonah's outright fury.

Eyes burning, throat tight, she managed to choke out a few more words. "I'm sorry. I'm so sorry."

"So am I." Shoving back from the table, he strode out after their son.

And as the door shut quietly behind him, the tears she'd fought back spilled over, unleashing what she knew would be an endless tide of grief that she'd brought entirely on herself.

9

By the time Grey made it outside, Jonah was already executing a multi-point turn to get his truck out from where it was trapped in the driveway between his and Rebecca's vehicles. He jammed his feet into his boots, not bothering to lace them as he bolted for the truck, slapping a hand on the hood.

Jonah scowled and rolled down the window. "I'm not going back in there."

"I'm not trying to make you. Just give me two minutes to move my Jeep so you don't rut up the yard."

Nostrils flaring, Jonah jerked a short nod.

Pausing only long enough to tie his laces, Grey trotted to his SUV and got behind the wheel. Rebecca's devastated face flashed in his mind. He didn't want to leave right now, but he was trained to handle emergencies in triage fashion. Jonah was the more volatile situation at this moment, so, for the first time in his life, he was going to see to his son. If Jonah would let him.

Feeling utterly ill-equipped to handle this, he scrubbed a hand down his face and backed out of the driveway, waiting for Jonah to do the same. When the truck peeled away from the curb with a squeal of tires, Grey followed. Jonah made no effort to shake him. Grey wasn't even sure he was aware he was being tailed. After about ten minutes of seemingly aimless driving, he finally figured out where the kid was going. The long gravel drive had been partly cleared. When he broke free of the corridor of trees, it was to see the bare patch of land where Rebecca's grandmother's house had once stood. Nothing remained of the structure or the foundation plantings that had circled it, save the burn pile that had been shoved off to one side to dry out.

Jonah was already out of the truck, pacing, hands laced behind his head, before Grey got his own vehicle parked. It was a good choice of location. If he needed to do some yelling about all this, there didn't seem to be any neighbors around to bother.

The younger man rounded on him as soon as he slid out of the Jeep. "Why did you follow me?"

Ignoring the hostility in the tone, Grey shut the door. "I wanted to check on you. I know you're not okay. Can't say I am either. Since we both got blindsided, it seems like a thing we should talk about."

"What good is talking going to do?" He could hear the thrum of pain beneath the words and hated it.

Moving over to Jonah's truck, he dropped the tailgate and sat. "Well, not talking about it hasn't gotten us anywhere good. So..." With an expectant stare, he gestured to the empty space beside him on the tailgate.

After a long, humming silence, Jonah dropped his arms and stalked over. He didn't sit. Instead, he braced himself, arms folded, on the side of the truck, looking across the bed. "I don't know what you want me to say."

Understanding he didn't want the intimacy of eye contact, Grey shifted and looked out at the night. "I don't *want* you to say anything in particular. But I figure there are things you need to say. Maybe all the reasons you're so pissed off, to start."

Jonah huffed out a breath. "I spent nearly my entire life believing that my father was basically a piece of shit who walked away from our family. Who didn't think we were worthy. And even though we found out last fall that the reason he walked away wasn't what we thought, it still wasn't good. He still wasn't the kind of man I could respect. That I could be proud to come from. He sure as fuck wasn't the father we deserved. We deserved someone who was fucking there. Someone who had spine enough to do the right thing. The hard thing. Someone who'd stand up for other people and not take the coward's way out. Because that's what everyone should fucking do."

God, how had he ever doubted that this was his kid?

Grey thought about everything Rebecca had told him about what Jonah had done after Lonnie left. How different would the boy's life have been if he'd simply manned the fuck up and talked to her all those years ago?

"It's what I should have done." The shame of it bowed his head.

"You didn't know. She made sure of that."

So much bitterness. He'd have to tread carefully here. "On one level, that's true. Objectively, I couldn't be there for someone I didn't know existed. But beyond that—and I know this in the deepest part of my gut—your mother didn't keep us apart out of some malicious intent. It wasn't that she didn't think I deserved to know about you or you about me. She was trying to do what she believed was best for everyone involved."

"How the fuck was this what was best?"

Grey twisted around to look at him. "Would you have made the best decision when you were eighteen and backed into a corner? I met you at twenty-three, and you were still plenty hot-headed. She was young. We both were."

Jonah scowled, reluctantly conceding the point. "I get why

she didn't say something then. I don't agree, but I get it. But she sure as shit should have told me later. After Lonnie left."

"And how would you have taken that news? Your whole world had just been up-ended. The only father you ever knew had just walked away. What would you have done if you suddenly found out, oh, hey, here's another one in the wings? I didn't know about you. Whether she'd told me or not, how would that have felt to you?"

The scowl got deeper, and Jonah blew out a breath. "Probably a lot like I feel right now."

"And how well would you have handled that at eight? You'd already been through something traumatic. I'd have been a stranger. Someone else who could disappear and disappoint you. She was trying to make sure it wouldn't get any worse."

He lifted his gaze to Grey's. "If she'd told you, you would have come."

It meant something to him that his son knew and believed that without hesitation. "I would have. But somehow, I don't think you'd have welcomed me. Just like I don't expect you to welcome me now. Despite the existing relationship we have, you didn't ask for this."

His throat worked. "Neither did you."

That hesitation absolutely killed Grey. "I didn't. But I'd be lying if I said I hadn't hoped for it."

"Really?"

For just a moment, he could see shades of the child Jonah had been, and he ached that he hadn't been here to carry the load he'd taken on at such a young age.

"I mean, not back then. The idea of having a child with Rebecca never even occurred to me after we split. But after I met you? It was hard not to think about all those what ifs and the life I walked away from."

Straightening, Jonah finally circled around to the end of the truck, sliding onto the tailgate. "You're awfully calm about all of this."

"I'm sure that won't stay the case once I really have time to think about it, but you don't need me losing my shit on top of you losing yours."

"Aren't you pissed about being lied to?"

"Like everything else with your mom, that's complicated. I thought I understood all my regrets for ending things with her. It's something I've carried a long, long time. But I'm realizing that all that is only the tip of an iceberg. And I'm gonna be thinking about that, carrying that, for a good long while." Grey twitched his shoulders. "But finding out today that there was even more for me to regret doesn't suddenly make her guilty and me in the clear. We both screwed it up."

He looked up at the star-studded sky, searching for the right words that might help salvage Jonah's relationship with his mother. "I don't agree with what she did. But I understand it. I can only imagine how scared she was, and I truly think she made the best decision she could under the circumstances. There was certainly never any opportune time to bring it up because when I did come back, I saw her pregnant, with Lonnie's ring on her finger, and I just couldn't face her. Not even for some kind of closure. So I left and stayed the fuck away for thirty years. That's on me. I don't know what would have changed, but that's on me."

With a sigh, he looked back at Jonah. "And then there's Lonnie. One of my closest friends, who tried to do the right thing in my stead, so I could go do the thing they both thought I wanted to do. There's a debt there that I can't repay. I know he fucked up, too. And I'm more sorry for that than I can say, because I know what that did to you. But that's all past. You and I both know there aren't any do-overs."

They fell into silence, and Grey wondered if Jonah was

feeling the cold. He sure as hell was, but he'd stay out here as long as his son needed.

When Jonah finally spoke again, the anger had bled out of his voice. "A part of me feels robbed of the family we could have had. The relationship we could have had."

Grey nodded. "I get that. But under the circumstances, we're lucky."

"Lucky?"

"Yeah. Despite everything, we aren't strangers suddenly sprung on each other. We have a relationship. Maybe it wasn't the one that either of us would've wanted or what we would have had if I'd come back sooner, but we've had a friendship and mutual respect for most of the last decade. We got to know each other independently of all this, and I don't take the gift of that for granted."

"There's something I don't understand. From what I gather, you basically carried a torch for Mom all these years. When you met me and realized who I was, who she was to me, found out she was divorced—why didn't you contact her then?"

He wasn't gonna quit asking the hard questions. Grey figured he had a lifetime of them to make up for, so he didn't try to evade.

"I nearly did. There was a part of me that wanted to hop on the next plane and show up on her doorstep. But I didn't know how I'd be received. You said she was divorced, but you never said much about her relationship status beyond that, and I couldn't ask you. And the longer things went on, the more I got to know you and started to wonder if you were mine, the more I thought about just showing up to find out the truth. But I was just as afraid of finding out the answer was no as I was of her rejecting me again. That would have been another disappointment on top of a whole boatload of disappointments that I didn't know how to take. So it was my own fear and cowardice that held me back,

stopped me from coming to get answers any sooner than I did."
Shifting toward him, he caught Jonah's eyes, needing him to hear
the truth in what he was saying. "I can't make up for that. I can't
change all the time and years we lost. But I hope you're willing to
entertain the idea of a relationship in the future. If you can't look
at me as a father, I hope you'll at least let me stay your friend."

Jonah's throat worked, but he nodded. "It does help."

"What does?"

"Knowing I come from you."

Grey's heart swelled with love and gratitude, and his own
throat went thick. He reached out and settled a palm on Jonah's
shoulder. "Thank you. That means a lot." Before the moment
could turn awkward, he squeezed once and let him go. "I don't
know about you, but my ass has just about frozen to your truck,
and you've got a fiancée who's worried about you. If you've
learned anything from our mistakes, go on home and talk to
your girl."

He winced. "I'm sure she'll have opinions about my
behavior."

"Probably. But she loves you, and you love her, so you'll
listen."

They both stood.

Jonah closed the tailgate. "Does this change things between
you and Mom?"

Grey shoved his frozen hands into his coat pockets. "I don't
know. I still need to think about the whole thing. It's a lot to
process, and she and I will need to talk after I've had time to do
some of that."

"For what it's worth, I hope you two can work it out."

One corner of his mouth tipped up. "Me, too. Go on and get
home. I'll talk to you later."

Jerking a nod, Jonah moved around and opened the driver's
side door. "Grey?"

"Yeah?"

"Thanks."

"Any time."

Already dreaming of the heated seats, Grey headed for his Jeep. As he slid inside, the phone in his pocket began to ring. He dug it out, expecting to see Rebecca's name pop up on the display. But it was Ned. Cranking the engine, he hit answer.

"Greyson."

"I've got us a meeting at The Pentagon tomorrow afternoon." Ned's excitement fairly crackled over the line. "You wanted the chance to pitch this to the brass, to get our program on the list. This is it. You need to get your ass to D.C. pronto."

He pinched the bridge of his nose.

Really? This has to happen now?

His personal life was in shambles, and he needed to talk to Rebecca. But in truth, this meeting could mean the difference between making his program a reality and failing spectacularly.

Failure wasn't an option for the future he wanted.

He shifted the SUV into gear.

"I'll be there. Text me the details."

SOMEWHERE DEEP DOWN, Rebecca had always known this would be the outcome of that desperate choice so long ago. She'd known, and she'd never had a clue how to stop the crash or even mitigate the damage. Now the secret that should never have been a secret was out, and she was deathly afraid she'd just lost both the men in her life.

After they'd walked out, she'd somehow found the strength and control to make it home, fending off Rachel's profound apologies. None of this was her fault; Rebecca had just needed to escape. To get to her own safe space, such as it was. She was pretty sure Rachel had driven behind her, just to see she arrived safely, though she hadn't been able to see much past the tears.

All her focus had been on the strip of road ahead, then on putting one foot in front of the other until she was through the door and into her own kitchen. She'd collapsed there, curling into a ball as a tsunami of what ifs threatened to drown her.

What if she'd told Grey from the beginning? What if he'd actually talked to her when he came back the first time? What if she'd told Jonah the truth when he was young? What if she'd sucked it up and told Grey on New Year's Eve? What if they both never forgave her?

She'd learned years ago not to waste energy on the what ifs. There was no going back and changing anything. She just had to move forward the best way she could. But she didn't know how to move forward from this. No apology on earth could make up for keeping the truth hidden all this time. That line could not be uncrossed. The betrayal couldn't be taken back. And, no question, her son saw this as a betrayal. Maybe Grey did, too. He'd become so self-contained, it was hard to tell where they stood. Would he understand what she'd done? Or was Jonah's father even more like him than she'd realized?

Time lost meaning as she huddled on the floor, weeping with regret. She might've lain there for minutes or hours by the time the doorbell rang. Heart leaping with hope, she scrambled to her feet, hastily wiping at her face as she stumbled to the front of the house to answer. Which one of them had come? No one else would be here this late.

She flung open the door, not sure who she was hoping for more.

Jonah stood on the front stoop, hands in his front pockets, shoulders hunched, looking considerably calmer than when he'd stormed out.

At the sight of him, Rebecca burst into tears again. "I'm sorry. I'm so sorry. I—"

He held up a hand. "Stop."

Though there was no bite to his tone, she snapped her mouth shut, terrified of what he was about to say.

He stepped inside the house and shut the door. So he didn't intend to leave immediately. That was good, wasn't it?

Those big, broad shoulders twitched on a long sigh, and he didn't quite meet her eyes. "It has been brought to my attention that I've been behaving like an asshat, and I'm here to apologize."

The statement surprised her enough to stop the tears, and for a moment, she could only blink at him. Was that acknowledgment Rachel's doing or Grey's?

"Let's sit."

Still silent, she followed him into the living room. When he took one end of the sofa, she cautiously took the other, hoping the fact that he hadn't taken the chair and the distance it afforded was a good sign.

He braced his forearms on his spread legs, lacing his fingers together in a gesture she recognized as a sign of him working his way up to something. He'd done the same thing when he'd sat her down to tell her he was becoming a SEAL. Would this be as terrifying? Would it be worse?

Rebecca fought not to mirror the pose as her own anxiety ramped up.

"All my life, you've been this constant. This solid, steady presence. I never had to think about you as anything other than my mother. And it's been pointed out to me how disrespectful I've been. First, over the idea of you getting into a relationship with Grey. And then losing my shit over the fact that you'd already had one, that I was a consequence of that, and storming out."

"You had a right—"

"I'm not finished. I said a lot of harsh things tonight, and you just took it. Like you took a lot of things in your life, trying to see that Sam and I were taken care of the best way you knew how. And that's what I expected. That's what I've always expected you to be. That stable, unchanging figure in my life, instead of a person in your own right. One who knows her own mind and sometimes makes mistakes. Somebody who has a right to go after what she wants, not just what I sign off on."

He finally lifted his head to meet her gaze with those eyes that were so much like hers. "I'm still angry. I still think I had a right to know—that we both did—a lot sooner than now. But I get that you were young and in a really tough position. I sure as hell can't say that I was making the best decisions at that age. So I'm working on processing the rest of it, and I wanted to say that I love you, and I'm sorry for how I behaved and how I reacted."

She wasn't losing him. As her biggest fear fled, Rebecca found a shred of the control that had deserted her. "Thank you. That means a lot." Wanting to give him something other than apologies or excuses, she swallowed. "I always wished I could tell you that your father—your real father—was a good man. You're so much like him. Always were. I'm sorry I never shared that with you before."

"It's weird that I know that. Hell, I saw it first-hand all the years I served under him. It does ease something in me, knowing I come from that."

Grateful he could find any comfort at all in this situation, Rebecca risked laying a hand on his arm and squeezing, hoping he didn't shrug her off.

"Did you love him?"

She should've expected the question. "Grey?"

"Both of them."

"As I said before, Lonnie was one of my best friends from childhood. I knew he had deeper feelings for me when we married. I loved him as a friend, and I grew to love him as more. But I was *in* love with Grey. I'm still in love with Grey. Not that it matters now." She fought back the wave of grief that wanted to pull her back under. "I don't know if it would have made a difference if I'd found some way to tell him sooner or in a more controlled fashion. It's not something you can just casually slip into a conversation."

Jonah dropped his head with a sigh. "I'm sorry for making it worse."

"No. No, you have a right to be upset, and I should have considered that more than I did. I was so caught up in trying to figure out how to tell Grey, and then... In the end, it didn't matter. As you said, there's no good way."

"Have you heard from him?"

"No." And at this point, she had no idea whether she ever would.

"For what it's worth, I think he still wants to try to work things out between you."

Was that true? Or was there some little boy part of Jonah who fancied the idea of his parents actually being together? Only time would tell.

"It's late. We've been through a lot. I should probably get home so you can rest and so I can assure my fiancée that I did, in fact, apologize."

Rebecca rose when he did, but hesitated short of trying to hug him. She didn't know if he'd welcome the contact or not. Jonah solved the issue by pulling her in himself, wrapping those big, strong arms around her. He'd towered over her for years now, but he still felt like her little boy, and she could still conjure the scent of him as a baby as she pressed her cheek to his chest.

"I love you, Jonah. All I've ever wanted is the best for you."

"I know. I love you, too." With one final squeeze, he stepped back. "Goodnight."

She followed him to the door and watched as he climbed into his truck. At least one part of her life was on its way back to rights. Whether the situation with his father would be any easier remained to be seen.

Had it only been last night that they'd come together and lost themselves?

Things had gone so wrong, so fast.

The faint ringing of her phone sounded from the kitchen. Racing back, she found it in her purse. Seeing Grey's name flashing on the screen, she fumbled to answer before it went to voicemail.

"Hello?" Nerves and fear made her breathless.

"Hey."

"Grey, I'm so sorry. I—"

"That isn't a conversation to be had over the phone."

"No, you're right." Did he want to come over? It was already so late, and she was so tired, she didn't know if she could cope with another round of emotional boxing.

But before she could respond, he went on. "I just wanted to let you know that I have to leave town for a bit, and I'm not sure how long I'll be gone."

Everything inside her froze. "I see."

The line echoed with the sound of vehicle doors closing.

"You're leaving now?"

"Yeah. I've got a meeting tomorrow. Can't afford to miss it." He sounded distant and disconnected.

"I see." And she did. This was his way of pulling back. Putting distance between them before he left for good.

"I'll be in touch."

"Okay."

"Bye, Rebecca."

"Bye."

With the sound of her name ringing in her ears, the line went dead.

She burst into fresh tears, knowing she'd never be lucky enough to win them both back.

When the brass he'd come to meet extended a hand across the desk, Grey took it. "I certainly appreciate you taking the time to meet with us and hear our pitch."

"This sounds fantastic. I know you'll take some time to get up and running, but consider yourselves on the list when you are."

"Thank you, Sir."

"Can't have enough programs to help our veterans with the transition back to civilian life."

"We couldn't agree more." Ned Maguire offered his own firm handshake. "We'll be in touch."

The pair of them filed out, making their way down labyrinthine halls and through security. Grey felt weird being back in Washington. Weirder still being in a suit instead of his uniform. He'd only been gone for a matter of months, but already the life he'd led for thirty years was starting to feel alien. Or maybe that was simply the exhaustion and emotional upheaval of the past twenty-four hours.

The moment they were out of the building, Ned burst into a

broad grin. "Well, I don't think that could have gone any better."

"No. No, that was exactly what we wanted."

One sandy brow winged up. "You don't seem as excited as I thought you'd be."

"Well, I was up all night driving to get here, so please excuse my lack of enthusiasm and energy. I think I used it all in the presentation. I'm pretty damn tired." And that fatigue went so much deeper than his friend could know. The two-hour nap he'd managed prior to their meeting hadn't done a damned thing to restore him. His dreams had been full of Rebecca.

Despite the necessity of his presence for this meeting, Grey knew leaving town last night was shitty of him. He knew that call he'd made had hurt her, which—despite everything —was the last thing he wanted to do. It had been more than obvious that she felt guilty about the whole thing, and she'd unquestionably suffered from the decision she'd made. He wasn't interested in punishing her for it because that wasn't who he was. So he'd spent the long drive processing and spinning through what ifs, trying to decide where they should go from here. Did this change things for him? Was this whole situation a sign that he needed to slow his roll and take a step back from her until things settled with Jonah? Or was it just another reason to go full-steam ahead on his original plan?

"Earth to Mitchell."

Grey blinked. "What?"

"Man, your head is off in the clouds. Is there something else going on with you?"

I found out I have a grown son with the woman I've been in love with most of my life. I'd say that qualifies as something going on. But he couldn't bring himself to talk about it with anyone else before he'd discussed things with Rebecca.

When he said nothing, Ned turned to face him. "Does this

have something to do with the other reason you went down there?"

"What are you talking about?"

"Oh, come on. The woman."

Grey stared at him. "I never said—"

"You didn't have to. I've known you for what? Twenty-five years? You always got this look any time you talked about Tennessee. I figured there was somebody. You've got that same look now."

When he only waited, Grey blew out a breath. He couldn't fault his friend for paying more attention than he might have wanted. No sense in denying the truth. "Yeah, it's about her."

They began walking again. "How are things going in that department?"

"Before yesterday, I would have said absolutely amazing." He'd finally had her back in his life, in his bed—metaphorically speaking. They'd been on the same page.

"Something happened?"

They'd hit an emotional landmine. "You could say that. I don't want to get into it." He was too damned tired and there was too much history that needed to be explained.

Ned nodded. "All right. But does this impact where you want to set the program? Because we're to the point where we need to be buying land."

Over the course of the meeting, an idea had begun to percolate in the back of Grey's brain in conjunction with all he'd been pondering on the drive up. "Yeah, I think it might. I've gotta get my ass back to Tennessee and do some checking. When I narrow it down to the contenders, do you want to come down and see, or do you trust my judgment?"

"I'm ready to move when you're ready, so your say goes. You find the property. I'm in for whatever."

"Okay. I'll let you know as soon as I know something."

"Sounds good." At their vehicles, Ned pulled him in for a

back-thumping hug. "It's good to see you, man. And I hope things work out whichever way you want them to."

"Thanks." Grey returned the thump. "I'll call you."

He waved his friend away and got into his Jeep.

The phone in his pocket began to vibrate before he cranked the engine. Maybe it was Rebecca. He fished it out, his spirits sinking a little when the Tennessee number flashing across the screen wasn't hers.

"Greyson."

"Captain. This is Magnolia Bradford."

After a moment of stunned surprise, he got his manners in gear. "Magnolia. I wasn't expecting to hear from you. How are you feeling?" That was the safe thing to ask after someone gave birth, right? She wouldn't be calling if something had gone wrong.

Her warm chuckle filled the line. "Tired, but happy to be home with the new little one. That's why I was calling, actually. To say thank you for the lovely baby gift."

"Oh, well, it seemed like the least I could do given the lengths you went to on my behalf when you were in labor. Um. What did you have?"

"A girl this go-round. Willow Elise. Eight pounds, thirteen ounces. Twenty-one inches. She's gonna be tall, like her daddy."

Was that a good weight and height? He had no idea. "Congratulations. I assume Calvin is a very proud papa."

"He is absolutely besotted. Right now, so is her brother. We'll see how long that lasts. How did you find the property I sent you to?"

Shit. With everything else that had happened, he hadn't actually had a chance to come clean about this part. "It was something of an adventure. We actually got trapped out there overnight by the ice storm."

"Oh my God!"

"It was fine. I had supplies in my Jeep, and we left the place as we found it, other than the ashes in the fireplace. I figured I'd explain to the owner and apologize. I'm happy to send any kind of reparations."

"No, no. I'm sure he'll be fine and grateful you were able to take shelter. Did that improve or destroy your opinion of the property?"

For a moment Grey had a flash of bare skin in firelight. Face heating, he cleared his throat, grateful she couldn't see him. "It certainly fits the parameters and is a solid contender. There's actually another property I'd like you to check on. Or rather, get your assistant to check on, if possible. I'm not aware if it being on the market, but I'd like to find out who owns it and whether they'd entertain an offer."

Her tone sharpened. "I'm intrigued."

He told her what he had in mind.

"Now I'm doubly intrigued. I don't know offhand who owns it, but I can certainly find out."

"You need to stay home and enjoy time with that baby. If your assistant can find this out quickly, great. But I don't want to interfere with your maternity leave." No matter how much he wanted an answer ASAP.

"Seriously, it would just take a phone call or two. No time at all."

"I heard that!" Calvin's voice echoed from the other end of the line.

Magnolia heaved a put-upon sigh. "That one's not gonna let me do anything."

"I heard that, too!"

"Please don't get in trouble with him on my account," Grey begged.

"Fine. I'll call my assistant and have her look into it."

"I appreciate it. We're basically to the point of being ready to make an offer somewhere. I just want to check on all the options."

"Understood. I'll—okay, Deena will be in touch as soon as we know something."

"Thanks, Magnolia. Now go enjoy your daughter."

"I certainly will."

Grey hung up the phone, wondering if he was out of his mind. Maybe. But the answer to his query just might determine what happened next.

In the meantime, he had every intention of falling into his bed at the hotel and not moving for the next twelve hours.

REBECCA PICKED at the crème brûlée that was the last course of the rehearsal dinner. The fact that she hadn't inhaled every bite of the magnificent meal prepared by award-winning Chef Athena Reynolds Maxwell was a damned tragedy. But at this point, she just didn't have it in her to do more than count down the minutes. She'd been aware of the looks everyone had shot her tonight. Word was starting to spread through the wedding party. That big new family had felt so warm and right at Christmas. Now she wasn't sure where she stood with all of them. No one had outright asked her about Jonah's parentage. She wouldn't have had a clue what to say if they had.

The last week had passed in a blur. She'd been able to lose herself in the million-and-one last-minute tasks surrounding the wedding. Mostly, it had kept her from dwelling on the fact that she hadn't heard a word from Grey since that brief phone call. She'd tried to embrace gratitude for the fact that her son was still speaking to her, and that he was adjusting to the new normal. Sort of. And Sam had taken the news better than expected. But the silence from Grey's quarter had been killing her. She wanted to believe that he would really come back. But deep down, a part of her thought she deserved it if he didn't. She'd kept his son from him. No matter her reasons, nothing could change that.

Rachel's family had arrived in town last night. Rebecca had done her best to put on a good face for them and everyone else in the wedding party. God knew, she had plenty of practice. But it was so damn hard. Harder than it had ever been. She'd really thought that, no matter what happened between the two of them, Grey would be back for Jonah's wedding. And maybe he would be. He could still show up tomorrow. For her son's sake, she hoped so.

For herself, she only wished for the night to be over, so she could go home, drop the mask, ditch the heels, and fall into her next round of crying with enough time to repair the damage before tomorrow's pictures.

The door to The Misfit Kitchen opened. Rebecca prayed it was more serving staff come to clear away the dishes. Her mind was on the cleanup when she realized the room had gone dead silent.

And she knew, without even turning her head.

"Dad. You made it."

At Jonah's words, her heart all but stopped. But she was still afraid to look.

"I didn't think you'd be here until tomorrow."

"I wrapped up the business I had going and wanted to come on this way."

At the sound of his voice, her traitorous heart began to beat again with a manic, hummingbird flutter. Looks were being exchanged all around, but Rebecca kept her focus on the half-eaten crème brûlée.

"Are you hungry? We could probably still scare up some dessert for you."

"That's not necessary."

Jonah shoved back from the table. "Let me introduce you to Rachel's family."

As they moved down the line, Rebecca chanced a glance in their direction. Grey was still dressed for the cold, in a black peacoat and plaid scarf. Everyone's face reflected the questions they were far too polite to ask. Her own questions burned in her throat, but she held them back. Now certainly wasn't the time and place. Well-bred Southern women did not make scenes, and she sure as hell wasn't going to do anything else to detract from Jonah and Rachel's special day.

"I need to steal your mother."

At the easy statement, Rebecca looked up in time to see some kind of silent communication going on between Grey and Jonah.

Jonah nodded. "We'll take care of your car, Mom."

"What?"

As Rachel appeared with her coat, it became clear that there'd been some sort of communication between them. "Don't worry about all this. We've got cleanup covered."

She'd been twisting in the breeze for the entire week, and he'd been talking with Jonah and Rachel? Resentment flared, then died again. She needed answers. She wanted absolution. Or, at the very least, resolution of some kind. With no idea if she'd get it, she took the coat and slipped it on. At least she'd get to see him one last time. That was more than she'd expected.

Grey held the door opened for her. She strode out into the night, hunching her shoulders against the chill. He said nothing as he led her around to his Jeep in the parking lot, opening the car door so she could slide inside. Those questions that had haunted her all week pulsed inside her, but she still didn't voice them. He was steering the ship at this point. He'd say what he wanted to say when he was ready to say it, and not before. It was maddening. A trait he shared with his son.

Not until they'd driven well past the city limits did she break and ask, "Where the hell are we going?"

"You'll see."

More miles rolled past until she couldn't hold her silence anymore. "Where did you go?"

"I had meetings in D.C., with a variety of folks, related to getting my program up and running. Everything's a go. We've bought some property."

"Where?" Had he bought the one he'd shown her?

As if reading her mind, he said, "We didn't end up going with the one where you and I spent the night."

Her heart twisted. Had she driven him away after all with her silence and secrets? If so, why was he taking her so far out of town?

"Seriously, Grey, where are we going?"

"Patience."

Tired, frustrated, and beyond emotionally wrung out, she snapped, "As you know, that's not one of my strong suits, and it hasn't gotten better with age."

His laugh rumbled in the SUV. The ease of the sound startled her. "I'm aware. We're nearly there."

He turned onto a gravel road she didn't recognize. She hadn't been paying a tremendous amount of attention to where they were going, and in the dark, she'd gotten a little turned around. She didn't recognize the gate he drove through. A tall, chain-link sort of deal, it was bigger than the one at the other place. Unlike that one, it was open.

Something about the terrain seemed familiar as they drove through the trees.

That can't possibly be right.

As the road wound out of the trees, the land opened up, and there it was. Stockton Quarry Lake. The water's surface was so still, it offered a near perfect reflection of the moon and stars above.

Her heart began to thunder, just being here throwing kerosene on a reluctant hope and making it burn bright. "Why did you bring me here?"

Grey still didn't look at her. "It seemed appropriate."

"Appropriate for what?"

He followed a winding road at the edge of a lake, toward a cabin. Its windows glowed gold, a welcome warmth against the cold winter night. "A conversation that's way overdue."

Parking at an overlook several yards from the cabin, he turned off the Jeep and slid out. She stared at the water, mind full of memories. By the time she brought herself back, he'd opened the door and offered his hand. Trembling, she placed her palm in his and slid out.

The warmth of his fingers wrapped around hers didn't settle her. Instead, the shaking worsened. Afraid she'd stumble as he led her toward the cabin, she dragged her feet. "What is this place?"

"Do you really want to have this conversation out here where it's colder than a well digger's ass in January, or do you want to be inside where it's warm?"

"I want clear answers, Grey. I need to know what you're thinking. Where we stand." Because if he'd brought her out here to break her heart again, she'd rather get it over with quick and clean like the death blow it would truly be.

On a sigh, he turned to face her in the moonlight, stepping close enough to brush the hair back from her face. "We're at a crossroads. This is where we started. There's a strong possibility it's where Jonah was started. And I want it to be where we start new. Start fresh. To build the family we never had the chance to build. No more secrets. Everything out in the open. I want us. I want everything we didn't have the chance for before."

It was everything she wanted and hadn't dared expect. But after the stress and strain of the last week, she didn't know how to believe him. "You don't hate me?"

His expression softened. "No." Realization seemed to dawn as he searched her face. "You thought I wasn't coming back."

Shame washed through her in a boiling wave. How many times did he have to prove himself? And yet, faced with the situation, with his silence, what else could she think? "Not for me. I wouldn't have blamed you."

"Seems like you've done enough of that for the both of us." He slid his arms around her, lacing his hands at the small of her back. "Do I wish you'd told me the truth when we were eighteen? Married me instead of Lonnie? Hell, yes. But I get why you did what you did. You don't have the market cornered on regret or blame in this situation. There were plenty of points where I could've made a different choice. But I can't overlook the fact that the choices I did make brought me back to you. That they enabled me to have a relationship with my son, despite everything. That feels like something of a miracle or Fate. I don't know. But I'll take it. We're still figuring out what our relationship is gonna be going forward, but he and I are good. So no, I don't hate you." He dropped his brow to hers, and that hummingbird in her chest lost its mind. "I still want you, Rebel. I still love you, and if you'll have me, have this place, we're yours."

Rebel. Maybe nothing else he could've said would've let her know he meant it. That they were headed back toward an even keel. Was she really this lucky? Was this kind, noble, stubborn man really giving her the second chance she craved? Did he really still want a life with her? It seemed he did. As the relief of that slid through her, weakening her knees, she struggled to parse out the rest of what he'd said.

"I don't understand. What does the lake have to do with it?"

Grey gestured with an expansive hand. "I bought it."

Rebecca's head kicked back. "You what?"

"I bought the lake and the three hundred acres surrounding. Everywhere we used to trespass and run wild. It's going to be the site of my new veterans intervention program. Well, part goes to that. There are about ten waterfront acres I carved out just for us. That's part of what took me so long. It wasn't technically on the market, and I had to go a fair bit above my original price range to convince the company that owned it to sell. Then my investors had to be sweet-talked into ponying up some more to cover the difference. But everything's been signed, sealed, and done. This cabin came with the property. It's not much. Just a sort of caretaker's cottage. But it'll do for now. If you want it. If you still want me."

This was it. Grey had put everything on the line. Laid everything out there about what he wanted, save for one thing. That part of the plan had been derailed because he hadn't managed to get her into the cabin yet. He wasn't a gambling man, but he realized that, in waiting to talk to Rebecca in person, he'd taken an enormous risk that her doubts would get the better of her. He thought he'd done enough to overcome those doubts for good, but she still hadn't given him an answer.

Tears glimmered in her eyes, shining in the moonlight. She swallowed hard and lifted her hands to frame his face. "I still want you. I still love you. God, how I love you. How I've always loved you."

Her words snapped the careful leash of his control, and he hauled her in, taking her mouth with his. Every pent-up fear and frustration of the past week rose up, needing release. Grey tasted the same desperation in her as she wrapped around him. With the last vestiges of sanity, he remembered they were outside in the freezing cold.

Tearing his mouth from hers, he gasped, "Not out here. Come on."

They stumbled toward the cabin. His hand shook as he unlocked the door and dragged her inside. Spinning her, he captured her mouth again, pressing her back and back until the door slammed shut and he had some kind of leverage. Rebecca whimpered, twining her arms around his shoulders, fingers diving into his hair. His own hands raced down, finding the backs of her thighs and lifting until those long legs circled his waist.

He could move quicker then, arrowing toward the full-size bed he knew was nestled in the corner. All the trappings he'd set up, all the effort he'd put into adding a layer of romance were going to waste, and he couldn't give a good damn. She'd notice later. After. Neither of them had the capacity for slow or savoring now. The need was too keen, desire too sharp. Nothing was more important than erasing the distance.

He tumbled her onto the mattress, following her down, his hands already working at her coat as she dragged at his. They shed clothes in a frenetic dance, seeking flesh. Touching, taking every inch they exposed. Her body was a fever as he plunged inside her. On a cry, she rose to meet him. For a moment they held gasping at the precipice, eyes locked and full of love and longing and relief. Then she shifted beneath him, urging him to move. Their pace was ruthless, brutal, as they strove to outrun all the stress and tension and pain that had haunted them for years. Her emerald eyes flashed as she held on, matching him stroke for stroke, until they arrowed past the edge of insanity and into a shattering release.

Grey came back to himself slowly, still gasping for breath. Rebecca lay beneath him, her arms still curled around his shoulders. That she could breathe at all with his weight pressing down on her was a minor miracle. As one of her legs slid limply down to the bed, he roused himself enough to roll to the side, bringing her with him. He wasn't ready to let her go yet. Or ever. She cuddled in against his chest, tangling her legs with his. As blood returned to his extremities, he managed enough muscle control to flip the edge of the comforter up to cover them. Mostly.

She pressed a kiss to his throat, and he tangled his fingers in her hair. "Well, I feel better."

Her unladylike snort rolled into big, bawdy laughter he couldn't help but find contagious. And here was the very last layer of release they'd needed. Everything in him felt cleansed and reset.

Abruptly, she stopped laughing and tried to sit up. "Grey."

"What? What's wrong?"

"Nothing. I..." She was looking around, taking in the cabin's interior.

It was one big open room, but for a bathroom in one corner. With some help, he'd decked the whole place out with flowers and electric candles. He'd even sprung for fancy new spa bedding. Not that they'd made it beneath the covers to test it out. He'd wanted to make it as romantic and appealing as he could, because he'd intended for tonight to be exactly what it was. A makeup and an apology. A new beginning.

"You did all this for me?" At the stunned wonder on her face, he vowed to give her as much romance as he could for as long as they had together. And he'd start by securing that forever.

"Yeah. We got a little out of the order of things. I meant for you to see all that first."

She settled back into his arms, resting her head in the crook of his shoulder. "You won't hear me complaining about the order of things. I feel like I could sleep for a week."

"If the sleeping is interspersed with more of all that, count me in."

Her fingers traced lazy patterns on his chest. "Well, put a

pin in that because I don't think either of those is an option for the immediate future. Our son's getting married tomorrow."

Our son.

It was the first time he'd heard her say anything other than "my son." The sound of it settled into him with a sense of rightness and gratitude.

"Yeah. Yeah, I know. The timing is maybe not ideal. But I wanted us to be on the same page before we went to the wedding."

"About us?"

"About us and also about how you want to handle the information about me. I know Jonah introduced me tonight to the wedding party, and word will get out sooner or later, but how do you want to handle it for the broader guest list?"

"I'm not ashamed, if that's what you're asking. Questions are bound to come up, and I'll take them as they come. But I don't want to do anything to overshadow Jonah and Rachel's day. That said, I think we leave it up to them. I'm not sure what Jonah will want to do."

"Well, there's one more thing that might influence his decision on that front."

"What's that?"

Extending his arm, Grey groped along the floor until he found his pants. It took a minute of digging before he managed to get his fingers on the ring he'd stashed there.

"I had planned this a bit differently, but you've brought me to my knees, metaphorically speaking, so I say it counts. I don't want there to be any mistake. Any question." He held out the princess cut diamond solitaire. "Marry me, Rebel. Make a family with me. Spend your future with me."

"Grey." Her voice shook, and those beautiful eyes went glassy again. Impatiently, she wiped at her cheeks. "Oh my God, how do I have any moisture left in my body to cry more?

Yes. Yes, I'll do all of that. And I will love you to the best of my ability for the rest of our lives."

He slid his ring on her finger and curled his hand with hers. "We've got a lot of lost time to make up for."

With a beaming smile, she kissed him. "I think we have just enough time to start on that before we have to head back to town."

"Thank God." And on a grin, he rolled her beneath him again.

REBECCA SMOOTHED sweaty palms down the skirt of her dress and took a breath before knocking softly on the door to the groom's suite at the church. A moment later, it swung open to reveal Brax in tux pants and an undershirt.

"Hey, Mama Ferguson."

"Y'all decent?"

"Close enough." He stepped back. "Come on in."

Self-conscious, she ran her thumb along the platinum band on her left hand as she stepped inside. She'd kept the ring turned stone side in since she arrived, and so far no one had noticed. Garment bags were hung hither and yon, with tux jackets and dress shirts peeking out. Jonah stood at a full-length mirror, fiddling with his tie.

He swung around to face her, his eyes searching hers. "You okay?"

His obvious worry about her erased a little of the anxiety. "Yeah." She smiled, wanting to put him at ease. "I just wanted to come talk to you for a bit before the ceremony."

"We can step out," Holt offered.

"No need. I actually wanted to talk to all three of you."

Her Momdar registered the faint traces of guilt in the looks they exchanged, and she figured they'd been recruited for at least part of Grey's plan.

"Did everything go okay last night? I'm sorry I let him ambush you. I thought—well, you needed to talk, and... I just need to know you're okay."

The conflicting loyalty in his eyes had her stepping forward, cupping his cheek with her right hand. "I'm fine, baby. Your father and I cleared the air." And God, what freedom to be able to call Grey what he was. "That actually leads to the thing I wanted to talk to the three of you about."

Holt and Brax moved in to flank Jonah, brothers in all but blood. Spinning the ring with her thumb, she smiled at their unified front and held up her left hand so the afternoon sun caught the stone. "We're getting married."

When none of them said a word, the nerves kicked back up again. With Jonah open to expanding his relationship with Grey, she'd thought he'd be okay with this. But maybe it was too much, too soon?

Before she could think what to say, he broke into a huge grin. "You said yes."

Holt sagged back against an armchair. "Oh, thank God. Cayla was gonna be so disappointed if the whole thing tanked."

"Wait, y'all knew Grey was proposing?"

"In broad strokes, yeah," Brax confirmed. "We helped get everything set up."

Jonah shoved his hands into his pockets. "We figured we'd done enough of the over-protective routine, and after the talk you and I had, I figured there was a solid chance his plan wasn't gonna blow up his face."

Rebecca didn't know how to feel about the fact that they'd all known what was coming. At the end of the day, it didn't matter. She'd gotten what she wanted. A second chance with the man she'd always loved.

Another soft knock sounded on the door.

Jonah kept his gaze on hers as he called out, "Come in."

Grey stuck his head inside. "Everything okay in here?"

"I was just getting confessions from your coconspirators." She reached out a hand, beckoning him inside.

"Don't get mad. I couldn't have pulled it off without them."

Her heart went to mush that they'd cared enough to help him when she knew their instincts were all about protecting her. "I'm not mad. I'm grateful. And my lipstick is the only thing saving all of y'all from big, messy, noisy kisses of thanks."

"How about hugs instead?" Brax suggested.

"That I can do. Come here, you." Because Brax was closest, she started with him.

Holt came next, his ice-blue eyes sparkling with humor.

Jonah rounded things out with a big squeeze. "I'm really glad y'all worked out. And that you can both be here today as my parents."

Rebecca fanned her face. "This mascara's waterproof, but damn it, don't test the limits."

Grey slid an arm around her waist and pulled her in, pressing a kiss to her temple. "Thanks. We both appreciate that."

When she thought she had herself under control, she sniffed. "I can take the ring off the rest of the day. We don't want to do anything to overshadow your day."

"No. You should absolutely wear it proudly. Tell everybody. You deserve it."

At the conviction in his tone, she teared up again.

"You mentioned this had something to do with us?" Holt asked.

Rebecca jumped at the distraction. "Oh, well, ordinarily, I'd have bridesmaids, but I'm kind of past that stage of my life. I'm asking Sam to be my matron of honor, but I was hoping that y'all would be my bridesmen."

All three of them puffed out their chests, their eyes going suspiciously shiny for a few moments.

Jonah swallowed hard. "I think I speak for all of us when I say, we'd be honored."

"Hell, yes," Brax added.

"It'd be a privilege," Holt echoed.

That led to another round of hugs and another wave of happy tears she had to fight off. Lord, she was leaking like a sieve.

"Okay, it's coming on close to time." Stepping forward, she reached for Jonah's tie, adjusting the ends. "I know you can do this yourself, but will you indulge me for today?"

"Sure. There's just one thing first." Looking to Grey, he straightened his shoulders. "This wasn't the original plan, but in light of recent events, it seems fitting. I was hoping you'd stand up there with me today as my best man."

Grey's face blanked with shock. His gaze darted to her for a moment of shared awe before turning back to Jonah. He knew as she did that this was a public claiming. She hadn't been aware Jonah intended to ask him, but she couldn't imagine anything more perfect.

Grey sucked in a shuddering breath. "There's nothing I'd like more." He offered his hand for a manly shake.

Jonah took it, hauling him in for a tight, back-thumping hug.

Damn it, they were really challenging the limits of this waterproof mascara.

Yet another knock interrupted the moment. Cayla called out from the other side. "Nearly time for places, y'all."

With one last sniff, Rebecca clapped her hands. "Okay, boys, y'all need to finish getting dressed. Jonah, let me get that tie."

Dutifully, they leapt into action, except for her baby boy, who now towered over her, standing still as a statue as she tied his tie for the most important day of his life.

"I love you, Mom."

Heart fit to burst, she indulged herself in one last hug before lifting her eyes to his. "I love you more. I'm so damned proud of you. Of the man you've become, and the woman you've chosen to spend your life with."

Patting the knot of the tie and adjusting his boutonniere, she forced herself to step back. "Congratulations, baby. I'll see you on the other side."

EPILOGUE

Grey drummed his fingers against his thigh, struggling not to tug at his bowtie or fidget with his cufflinks. His body fairly vibrated with restless energy and a need to *move*. He was ready to get this show on the road.

A big hand clapped him on the shoulder. "Chill out, Dad. It's almost time." Jonah's eyes were full of sympathy and amusement.

Grey didn't think he'd ever tire of hearing "Dad." All in all, the transition for the two of them had gone pretty smoothly. They'd built on their previous foundation and deepened their relationship.

"Hard to chill. I've been waiting my whole life for this." He'd been waiting his whole life for her.

"I get it. And from recent experience, let me just say you'll feel a thousand times better in approximately half an hour." He gestured back toward the row upon row of white chairs flanking a flower-strewn aisle.

Seeing that most of the seats were full, Grey had a moment

to wish he'd suggested eloping to the beach. He'd have been perfectly content with a small family affair. But their wedding was a big celebration, and it seemed everyone in town had turned out for it. In addition to the locals, a few dozen friends he'd made over the years had come down for the occasion, including the men who stood up with him today.

Ned slung an arm around his shoulders and turned him back toward the lake. "Here, let's focus on all that progress being made on our facility over there. The contractor said it should be ready for punch-out work by the end of the summer. We could be opening our doors by October."

Marcus Gaffy crossed arms still beefy with muscle, despite his near decade out of the Navy and the SEALS. "Gonna be a hell of a program when you're done. It's a beautiful spot for healing."

It sure as hell was. He and Rebel had done their own healing here in the months since Jonah's wedding. And as it had been the site of so many of their firsts, when she'd suggested having their wedding here, Grey hadn't been able to say no.

"That's what we're hoping." Appreciating the distraction, he turned his focus on Marcus. "You given any more thought to coming in as a guest instructor?"

"I reckon I could make that work." He grinned, his smile flashing bright in his weathered face. "Hell, it'd be worth the trip down just to see you in the role of grandpa."

"Never saw anybody quite so uncomfortable around babies," Alonso Moretti added.

"I'm getting better," Grey protested. Rory had seen to that. Now that she was mobile, she came toddling over to him every time Sam and Griff came to town, demanding to go "Up!" Rebecca insisted it was because she believed everyone would adore her. Grey secretly wondered if she could smell fear.

Jonah chuckled. "You'll have plenty of practice by the time ours gets here."

He wasn't wrong. Aside from Rory, Cayla and Holt's son would be arriving at the end of June. Rachel was due right around Christmas. Rebecca was utterly ecstatic.

Grey shot his son some side eye. "You're way too calm about this."

"Oh, I'm freaking out on the inside. Make no mistake. It's just hella fun to tease you."

"The secret," Jim Heneghan announced, "is to never let them see you sweat."

"He does know we're talking about babies and not interrogation by enemy combatants, right?" Marcus asked.

Jim shrugged. "Same applies."

Cayla circled around to join them, her brows firmly near her hairline. "I don't even want to know." She rubbed at the mound of her baby belly. "It's about time. Y'all need to get into place. Jonah, you come on back for the processional."

"Yes, ma'am. Dad, see you on the other side."

As his son disappeared to wherever the other half of the wedding party was gathered, Grey took his position at the front of the aisle. His friends assumed theirs, sentry to the celebration to come. Then the music started, and the audience turned en masse to watch the procession. Ripples of laughter spread through the crowd as a grinning Brax headed up the procession, bouquet in hand as the first of Rebel's bridesmen. Holt followed, then Jonah. Sam brought up the rear, beaming in a dress of deep rose. One by one, they all lined up on Rebecca's side. Then the music shifted, and Cayla and Holt's daughter, Maddie, and Mia and Brax's daughter, Dakota, flitted their way down the aisle, spreading flowers as they went. There really was no other word for it, as the pair were wearing fairy wings and flower crowns with trailing ribbons. Dakota's little brother,

Duncan, wore a serious expression as he barreled his way down the aisle at double time, ring pillow clutched in his little hands. Jonah, Holt, and Brax all crouched to give him a high five before he took up a hiding spot behind Brax's knees.

The music died out, and it seemed everyone took a collective breath before "The Bridal March" began to play. Everyone stood and turned.

And there she was, gliding down the aisle in a stunning white dress and glittering crown, with what seemed an ocean of flowers in her arms. Grey's breath simply wheezed out at the sight of her. She was radiant. Gorgeous. Perfect.

Rebecca reached the head of the aisle and took his hand, her fingers strong where they wrapped with his. Grey felt the nerves settle, and he wondered how he could've waited so damn long to make her truly his. Because this was exactly what he wanted, exactly where he was supposed to be. Everything in his life had finally come full circle, back to this. To her. To them.

He didn't remember the ceremony. Didn't remember repeating the vows the minister fed him. But he memorized the reflection of the lake in her stunning green eyes. The strand of hair the breeze teased out of her up-do. The sound of her confident voice declaring, "I do."

The moment they were announced "man and wife," time snapped into focus again. Finally cleared for some kind of action, Grey swept her into his arms, bending her back in a dip as he kissed his wife for the first time to the rousing cheers of the assembly.

She was laughing as he brought her vertical again. That uninhibited, joyful sound that would never grow old.

The cheerful recessional music began to play, and they made their way down the aisle, arm in arm, as their guests rained flower petals over them.

Rebel bent her head toward him as they rushed through the flurry of petals. "*Now,* will you tell me where we're going for our honeymoon?"

Pulling her close to his side, he asked, "How do you feel about Scotland?"

BONUS EPILOGUE

"A good meal in a Highland pub seems like a fitting end to two glorious weeks in Scotland." Rebecca laced her fingers with Grey's as they strolled down the high street in the village of Glenlaig in search of sustenance.

"I hope we'll be able to get one. Seems like there's something going on."

Cars lined the street and there seemed to be an unusual number of people out and about for a village this size. At least, compared to the others they'd traveled through over the course of their honeymoon. Grey had seen that they'd taken the road less traveled, exploring the parts of Scotland that weren't on all the tourist maps. Rebecca had loved every minute.

A carved wooden sign stuck out from a two-story stone building. *The Stag's Head.*

"This seems promising." Grey pulled open the door and held it for her.

As her eyes adjusted to the dark, she realized the interior was packed with people. "Might be awhile. Do we have time?"

"Sure. Our flight's not for another seven hours. We can wait."

A middle-aged woman with silver-streaked red hair pulled into a braid came bustling by, a pitcher of beer in her hand. "Table for two in the far corner there. Be with you when I can."

They navigated their way through the crowd to the tiny table next to the end of the bar. She stripped off her coat and settled into the chair, letting the cacophony of voices wash over her in a delightful muddle of Scots accents. They'd heard so many on this trip, and she'd been fascinated by the wild variance over such a small geographic area. As she scanned the laminated menu, she tried to identify what she was hearing.

"Sure, and you'll be wanting the fish and chips or the steak pie."

She glanced up at the old gentleman at the bar. He wore a kilt and a tweed jacket. A hat—oh, what had she learned they were called? A tam?—in the same plaid sat on the bar beside him. His hair was a shock of white, thinning on top, but the blue eyes he turned in their direction were sharp.

"Are those the house specials?"

The old man nodded. "Reliable as the sun, they are. And plentiful, which is helpful with the rush."

She stuck the menu back between the salt and pepper. "What's going on? We noticed all the people."

"Oh, well, we're just having a wee ceilidh to celebrate an upcoming wedding."

If this was a "wee" party, Rebecca couldn't imagine a big one.

"Somebody important in the area?" Grey asked.

The old man turned on his stool to face them, a half-drunk pint in his hand. "Well, you could say that. It's a three-hundred-year-old marriage pact that's finally being fulfilled."

Rebecca goggled. "Three hundred years! How does that work?"

"Well, it's like this, you see. Around four hundred years ago—"

"Three-hundred eighty-nine!" someone else piped up.

The old man rolled his eyes. "As I said, around four hundred years ago, a lad named William Lennox won the favor of the king."

Delighting in the obvious start to a story, Rebecca shifted toward him. "How'd he do that?"

"Saved his life, he did. Rescued him from being skewered by a wild boar. The king was, as you might expect, grateful for William's intervention, and he granted him lands in the area and a title of Baron to go with them."

"That's a hell of a boon," Grey observed.

"Aye, it is. Now, as you may be aware, this area belongs to Clan MacKean. Their holdings go back nearly nine-hundred years and were passed down from laird to son all that time. Now Robert MacKean, the laird at the time, had no respect for William Lennox. He was a farmer who got lucky with that boar. What did he know of running an estate? William, as you might expect, didn't appreciate the lack of recognition from the MacKean and so a feud was started. It went on for a few generations before the heads of the respective families decided there'd been enough bloodshed. They signed a marriage pact stating that the marriageable heirs on either side would wed and end the feud."

"A classic marriage for political reasons." She nodded, understanding. "But how is it that it's only just now being fulfilled?"

"Ah, well, that's the thing. Once the pact was signed, a series of accidents, mortal illnesses, and flukes of birth befell the families. Of those heirs who lived, all of a particular generation were the same gender for the past three centuries. Until now. It's become something of a legend around these parts, so the fact that the MacKean son and the Lennox daughter have made it this close to the altar is big news and cause for a village-wide celebration."

"Wow." Rebecca's romantic heart wanted to swoon a little, but she was too practical for that. "Do the bride and groom actually *want* to get married?"

"Want's got nothing to do with it. They've known all their lives that this was their duty. If they dinnae go through with it, both estates revert to the crown."

"Angus, quit bending their ears." The red-headed server stopped by their table. "What can I get you?"

They ordered fish and chips and pints of the local beer. By the time the server walked away, Angus had wandered over to join a group on the far side of the pub.

A little sad not to have more of the story, Rebecca turned back to Grey. "Can you imagine being caught up in an arranged marriage in this day and age?"

"I definitely would not want that hanging over my head. Talk about baggage. But maybe if they've known each other all their lives, and known this was coming, they're good with it."

"Maybe." She couldn't help but feel sorry for this bride and groom who seemed to have had their choices cut off merely by the circumstances of their birth. Real life was a far cry from the historical romances that made arranged marriages seem like a good idea.

The food, when it came, was excellent. After they'd finished, Grey paid their bill and helped her on with her coat. They stepped out of the pub, into the summer sunshine that was so much cooler here than in Tennessee.

Grey paused, smiling down at her. "Are you ready to head home?"

"Definitely not. It's been an amazing two weeks, and I'm not quite ready for the honeymoon to end. But we've got a flight booked, anyway, and the plane's taking off tonight, one way or the other."

He slid his arms around her, drawing her in for a lingering kiss. "Gotta get back to real life sometime. But we'll do this again. I want to show you more of the world."

"I'm holding you to that, Captain Greyson."

His eyes sparkled. "Anything you want, Mrs. Greyson."

They strolled arm-in-arm down the high street toward where they'd parked their little rental car. Footsteps sounded behind them on the cobblestones, coming fast.

Rebecca looked back to find a young woman with a panicked expression rushing toward them, a small suitcase in her hand and a backpack slung over one shoulder. She was dressed as any tourist might be, but something about her manner belied that impression.

"I'm sorry, but I couldn't help but overhear. You're headed to the airport?" Her voice carried a soft Scottish burr.

Grey tensed a little, shifting into what Rebecca had come to realize was action mode. "Yes. In Glasgow."

She cast a furtive glance around. "I realize this is a strange request, but is there any possible way I could hitch a ride?"

Rebecca stepped toward her. "Honey, are you in trouble?"

The blonde exhaled slowly, then squared her shoulders. "Yes."

"What's your name?"

"Afton Lennox."

Lennox. Rebecca would've laid money that this was the intended bride, and she definitely didn't look like she wanted to go through with the wedding. There were consequences for that, but it sure as hell wasn't their place to judge. All Rebecca saw in this moment was a frightened woman making a desperate choice. She understood what that was like.

Looking back to her husband, she made a silent plea with her eyes.

Grey unlocked the car. "Get in."

THANK you for reading this conclusion to the Bad Boy Bakers series! I know you're eager to find out what's next. I'll give you four hints:

1. It involves my favorite country in the world.
2. It was totally supposed to be a standalone.
3. It's definitely NOT a standalone.
4. It involves a bunch of hot guys in kilts.

That's right! We're jumping across the pond to go hang out in the Highlands of Scotland for a while in my new upcoming Kilted Hearts series! The prequel, *Jilting the Kilt*, drops November 18th and will be free everywhere ebooks are sold!

Arranged marriages are so three centuries ago. But that doesn't stop Afton Lennox from being bound by one. All her life she's been pledged to wed Connor MacKean. It's the only way to save both their families' estates, and they're friends, after all, so it won't be that bad. Right?

Hamish Colquhoun has spent his entire adult life trying to find a way to liberate his best friend from a marriage he doesn't want. If it also spares the woman he's secretly loved for years, it's of no mind to him. He's already got a wife and family of his own. Freeing them both is just the right thing to do.

But with the wedding just days away, time is running short. Afton and Connor are prepared to do their duty, fulfilling the pact made by their long-dead ancestors. There's one option Hamish hasn't mentioned. It would only buy some time at best and risk everything at worst. But as Afton begins to question everything, Hamish finds he can't stay silent.

God save them all.

BE sure to sign up for <u>my newsletter</u> so you don't miss its release!

And you can already preorder *Cowboy in a Kilt,* Book 1 in the Kilted Hearts series!

A cowboy without a home

Robbed of the family ranch that should have been his legacy, Raleigh Beaumont is a man with no roots and no purpose. When a friend drags him to Vegas, he figures he's got nothing to lose. But after a hell of a lot of whiskey and a high stakes poker game with a beautiful stranger, he finds himself the alleged owner of a barony in Scotland.

An heiress with a crumbling heritage

When her brother's bride disappears just days before the wedding that's meant to save their ancestral home from the mad marriage pact that's held their family captive for generations, Kyla McKean believes they've been granted a reprieve. Until she finds out about the new, single—male—owner of Lochmara and knows she's next on the chopping block or ownership of both their estates reverts to the crown.

A modern answer to a three-hundred-year-old problem.

Raleigh's lost his land once. He's not about to lose it again. Not even because of some lunatic pact made centuries before he was born. Kyla's desperate to save Ardinmuir. She agrees to marry him on one condition: They wed for one year to satisfy the pact, then get a quick and quiet divorce. There's no stipulation against it, and they'll both get what they want.

But this displaced Texan and his fiery bride are about to find so much more than they bargained for.

Cowboy in a Kilt releases January 13, 2023, so preorder your copy today!

OTHER BOOKS BY KAIT NOLAN

A complete and up-to-date list of all my books can be found at https://kaitnolan.com.

∼

THE MISFIT INN SERIES
SMALL TOWN FAMILY ROMANCE

- *When You Got A Good Thing* (Kennedy and Xander)
- *Til There Was You* (Misty and Denver)
- *Those Sweet Words* (Pru and Flynn)
- *Stay A Little Longer* (Athena and Logan)
- *Bring It On Home* (Maggie and Porter)

RESCUE MY HEART SERIES
SMALL TOWN MILITARY ROMANCE

- *Baby It's Cold Outside* (Ivy and Harrison)
- *What I Like About You* (Laurel and Sebastian)
- *Bad Case of Loving You* (Paisley and Ty prequel)

- *Made For Loving You* (Paisley and Ty)

MEN OF THE MISFIT INN
SMALL TOWN SOUTHERN ROMANCE

- *Let It Be Me* (Emerson and Caleb)
- *Our Kind of Love* (Abbey and Kyle)
- *Don't You Wanna Stay* (Deanna and Wyatt)
- *Until We Meet Again* (Samantha and Griffin prequel)
- *Come A Little Closer* (Samantha and Griffin)

BAD BOY BAKERS
SMALL TOWN MILITARY ROMANCE

- *Rescued By a Bad Boy* (Brax and Mia prequel)
- *Mixed Up With a Marine* (Brax and Mia)
- *Wrapped Up with a Ranger* (Holt and Cayla)
- *Stirred Up by a SEAL* (Jonah and Rachel)
- *Hung Up on the Hacker* (Cash and Hadley)
- *Caught Up with the Captain* (Grey and Rebecca)

WISHFUL ROMANCE SERIES
SMALL TOWN SOUTHERN ROMANCE

- *Once Upon A Coffee* (Avery and Dillon)
- *To Get Me To You* (Cam and Norah)
- *Know Me Well* (Liam and Riley)
- *Be Careful, It's My Heart* (Brody and Tyler)
- *Just For This Moment* (Myles and Piper)
- *Wish I Might* (Reed and Cecily)
- *Turn My World Around* (Tucker and Corinne)
- *Dance Me A Dream* (Jace and Tara)
- *See You Again* (Trey and Sandy)
- *The Christmas Fountain* (Chad and Mary Alice)

- *You Were Meant For Me* (Mitch and Tess)
- *A Lot Like Christmas* (Ryan and Hannah)
- *Dancing Away With My Heart* (Zach and Lexi)

WISHING FOR A HERO SERIES (A WISHFUL SPINOFF SERIES)
SMALL TOWN ROMANTIC SUSPENSE

- *Make You Feel My Love* (Judd and Autumn)
- *Watch Over Me* (Nash and Rowan)
- *Can't Take My Eyes Off You* (Ethan and Miranda)
- *Burn For You* (Sean and Delaney)

MEET CUTE ROMANCE
SMALL TOWN SHORT ROMANCE

- *Once Upon A Snow Day*
- *Once Upon A New Year's Eve*
- *Once Upon An Heirloom*
- *Once Upon A Coffee*
- *Once Upon A Campfire*
- *Once Upon A Rescue*

SUMMER CAMP
CONTEMPORARY ROMANCE

- *Once Upon A Campfire*
- *Second Chance Summer*

ABOUT KAIT

Kait is a Mississippi native, who often swears like a sailor, calls everyone sugar, honey, or darlin', and can wield a bless your heart like a saber or a Snuggie, depending on requirements.

You can find more information on this *USA Today* best selling and RITA ® Award-winning author and her books on her website http://kaitnolan.com.

Do you need more small town sass and spark? Sign up for <u>her newsletter</u> to hear about new releases, book deals, and exclusive content!

9 781648 350894